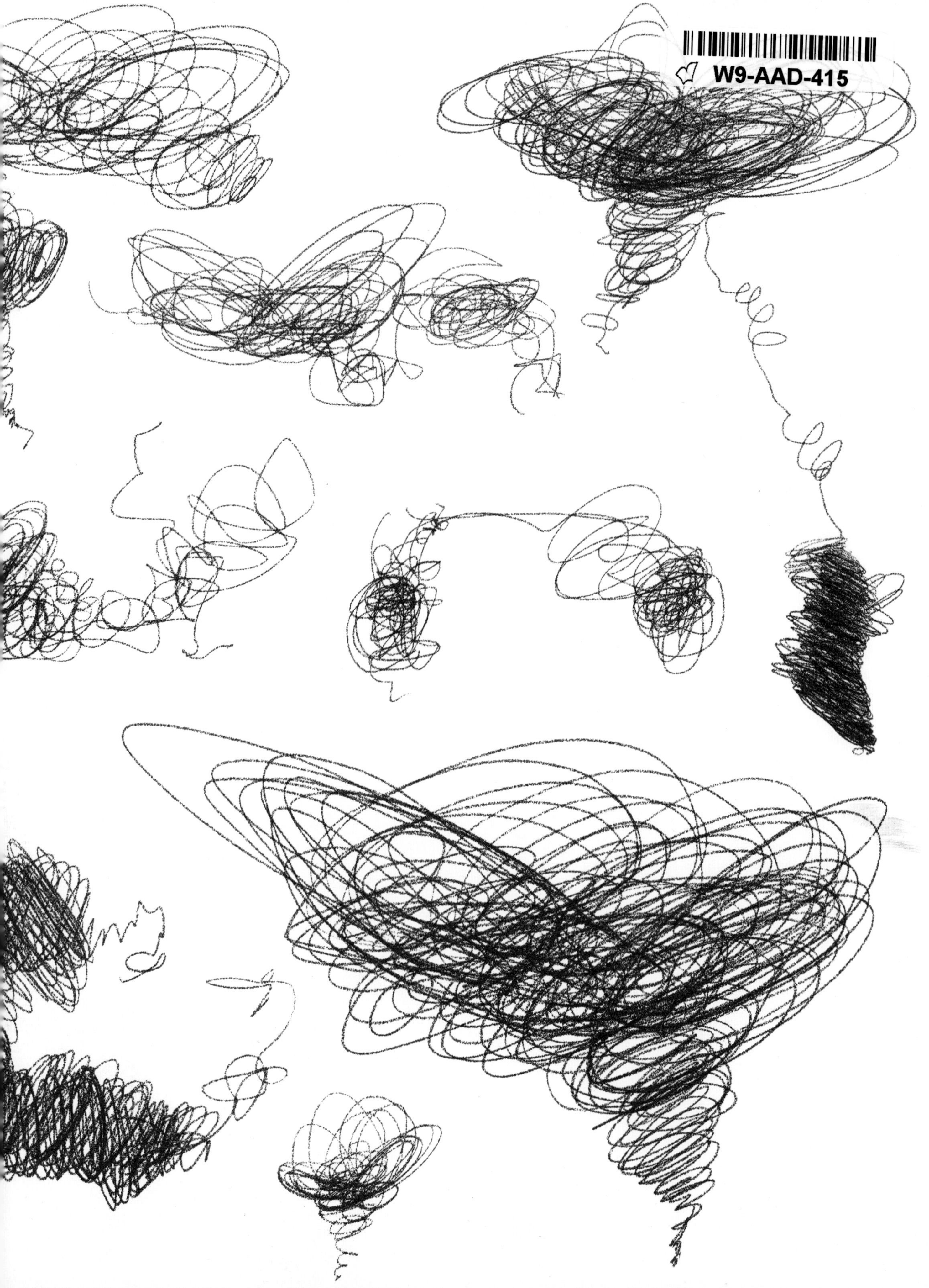

www.FlowerpotPress.com
DJS-0912-0184
ISBN: 978-1-4867-1556-5
Made in China/Fabriqué en Chine

THE BRAIN STORM

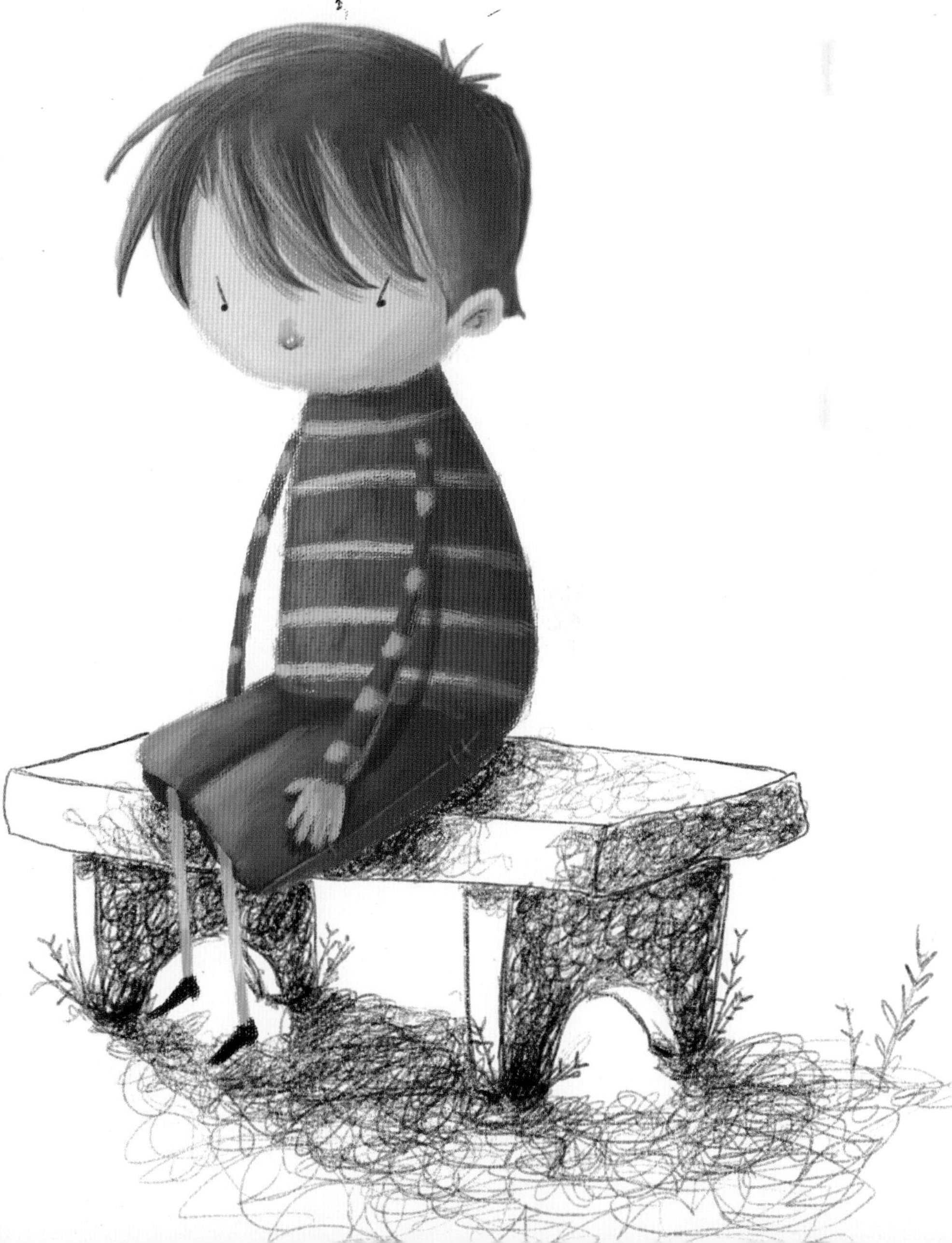

Unwritten by Linda Ragsdale
Illustrated by Claudio Molina

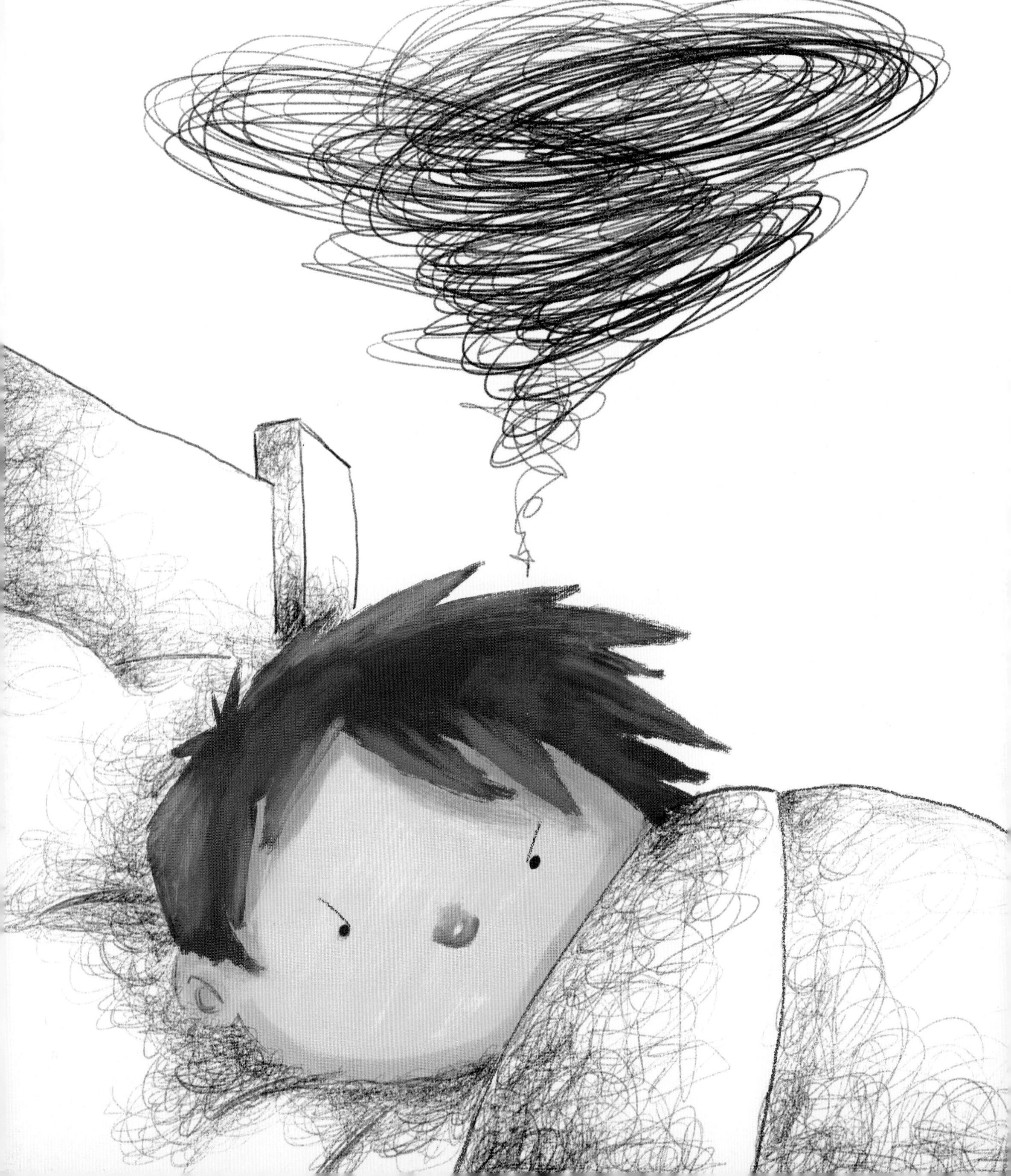

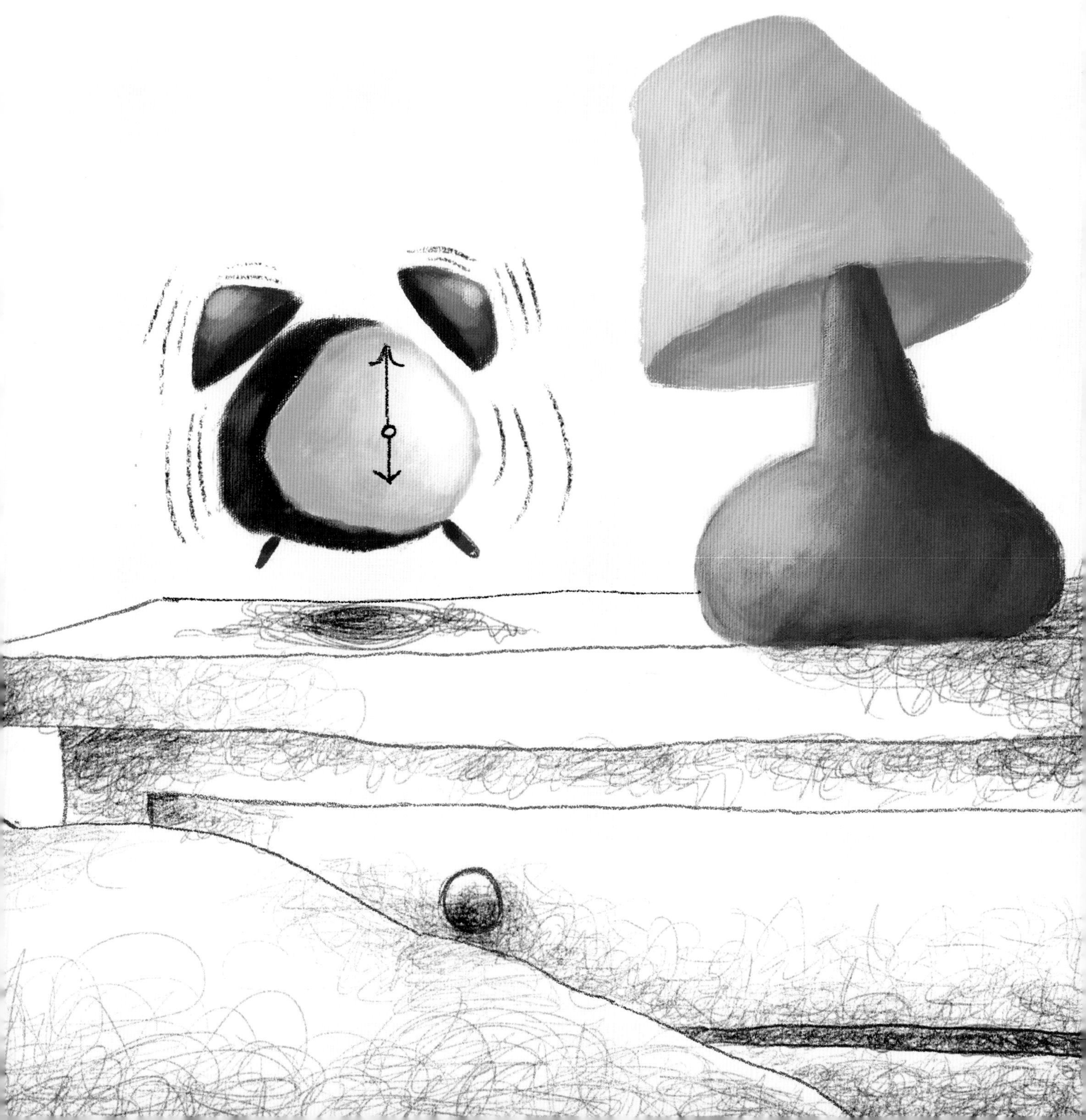

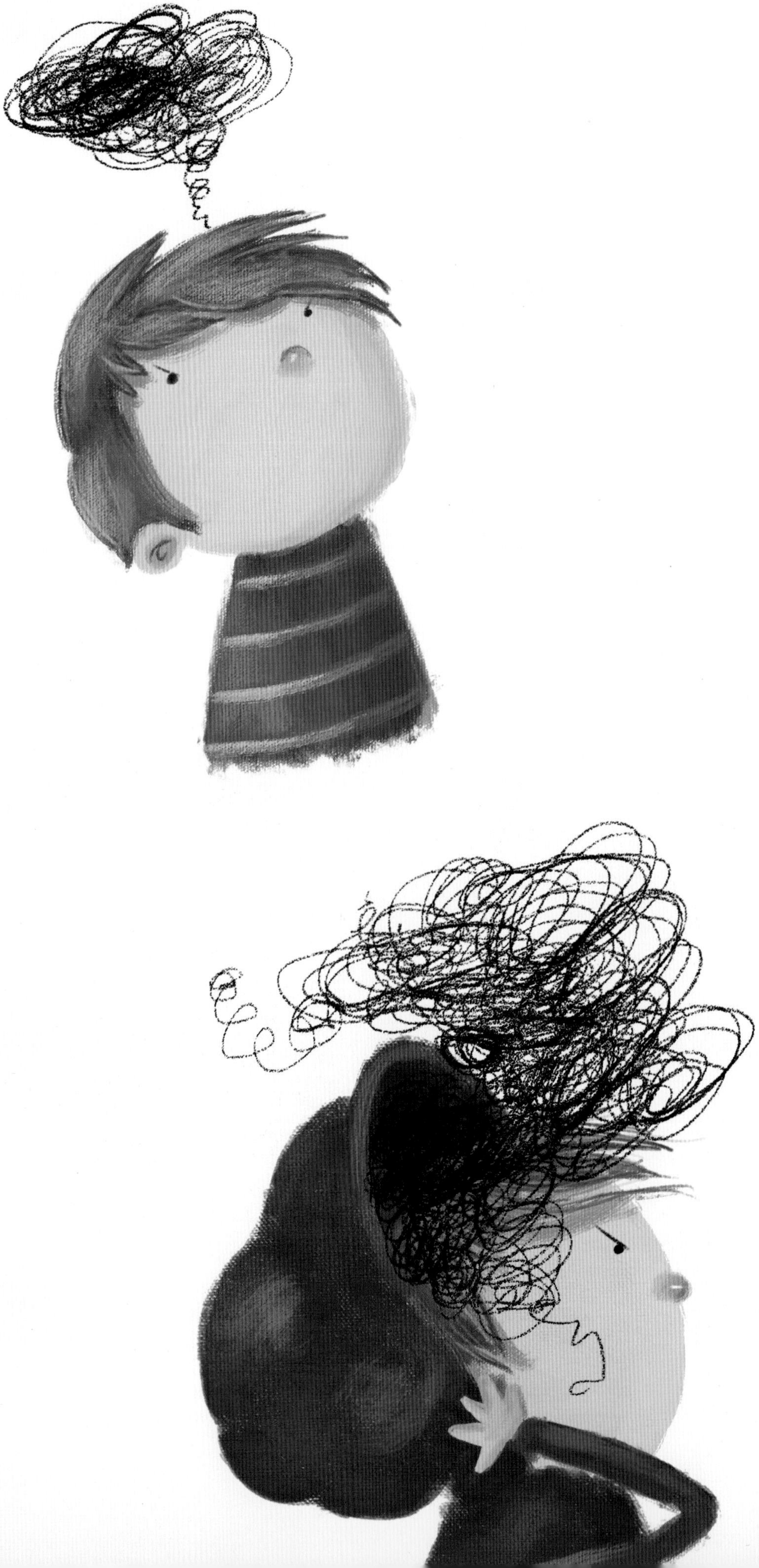

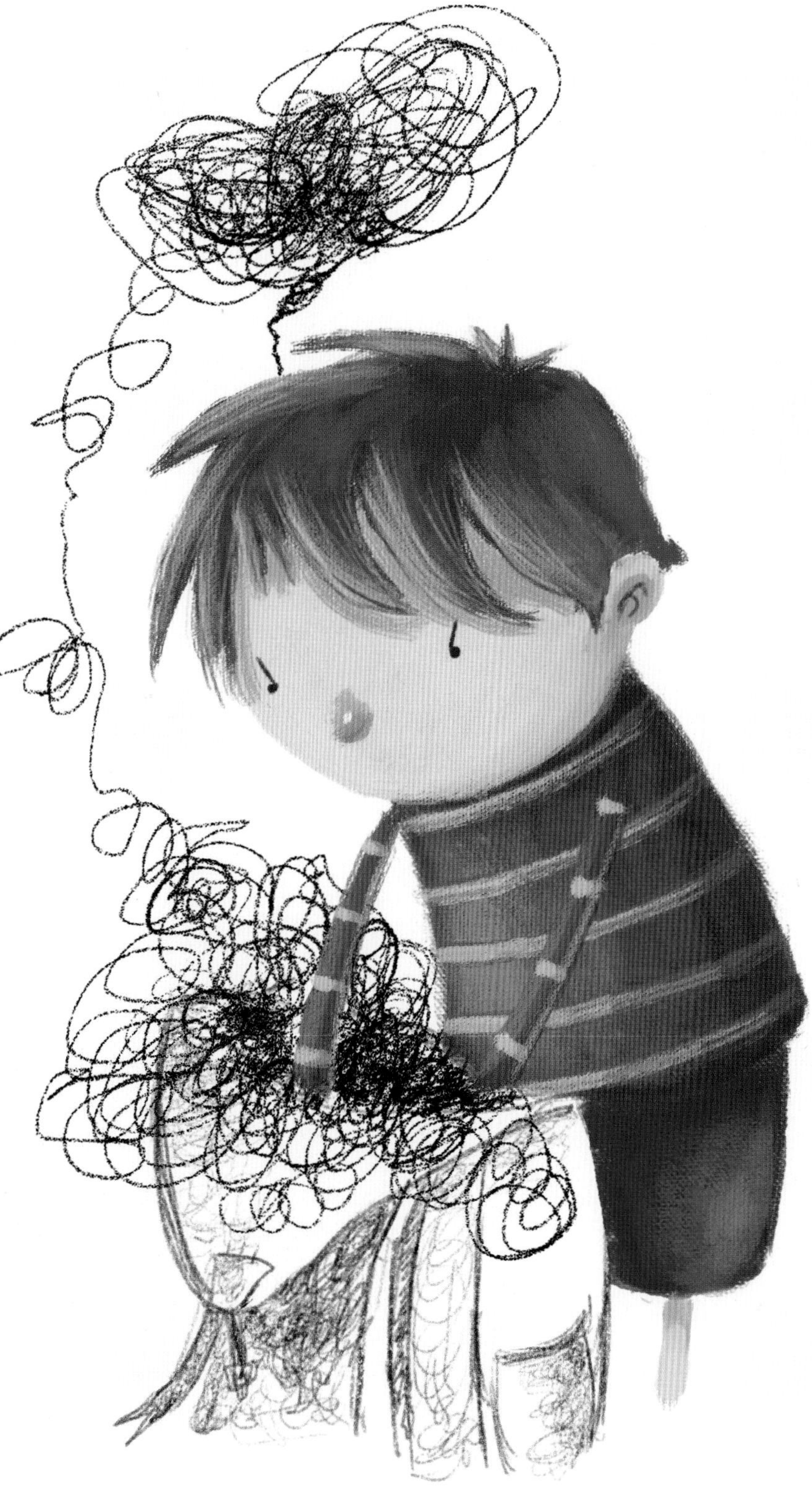

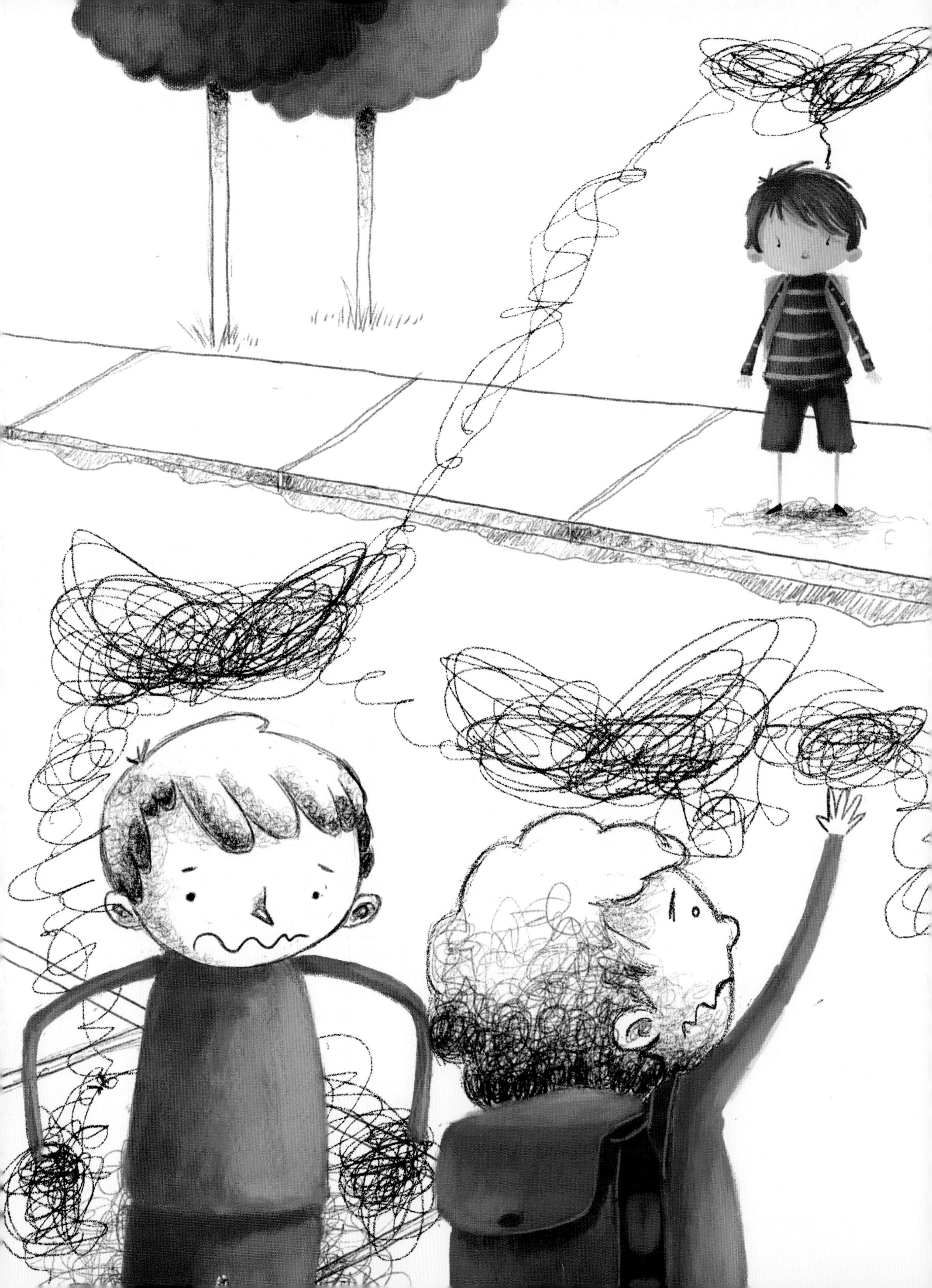

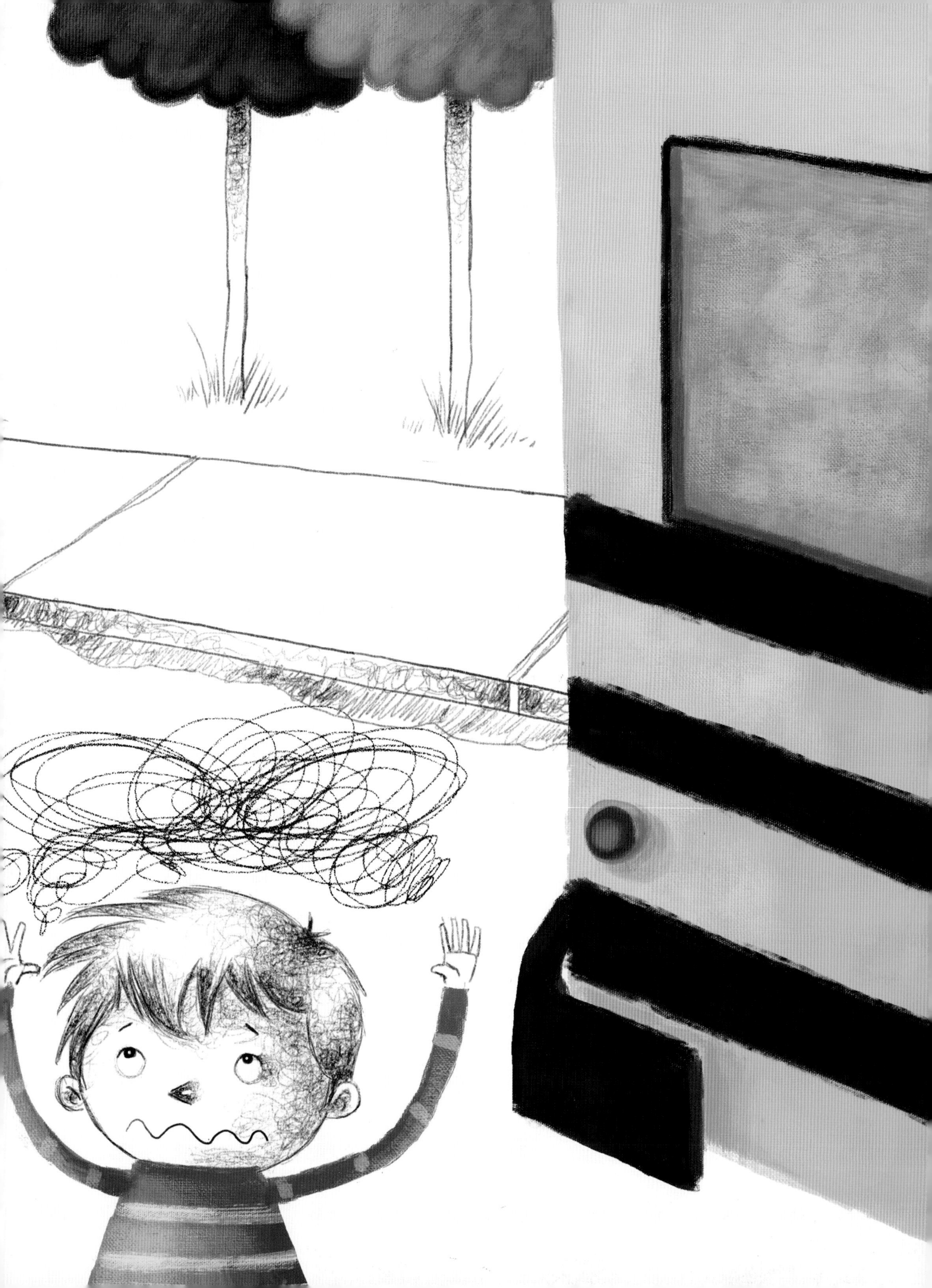

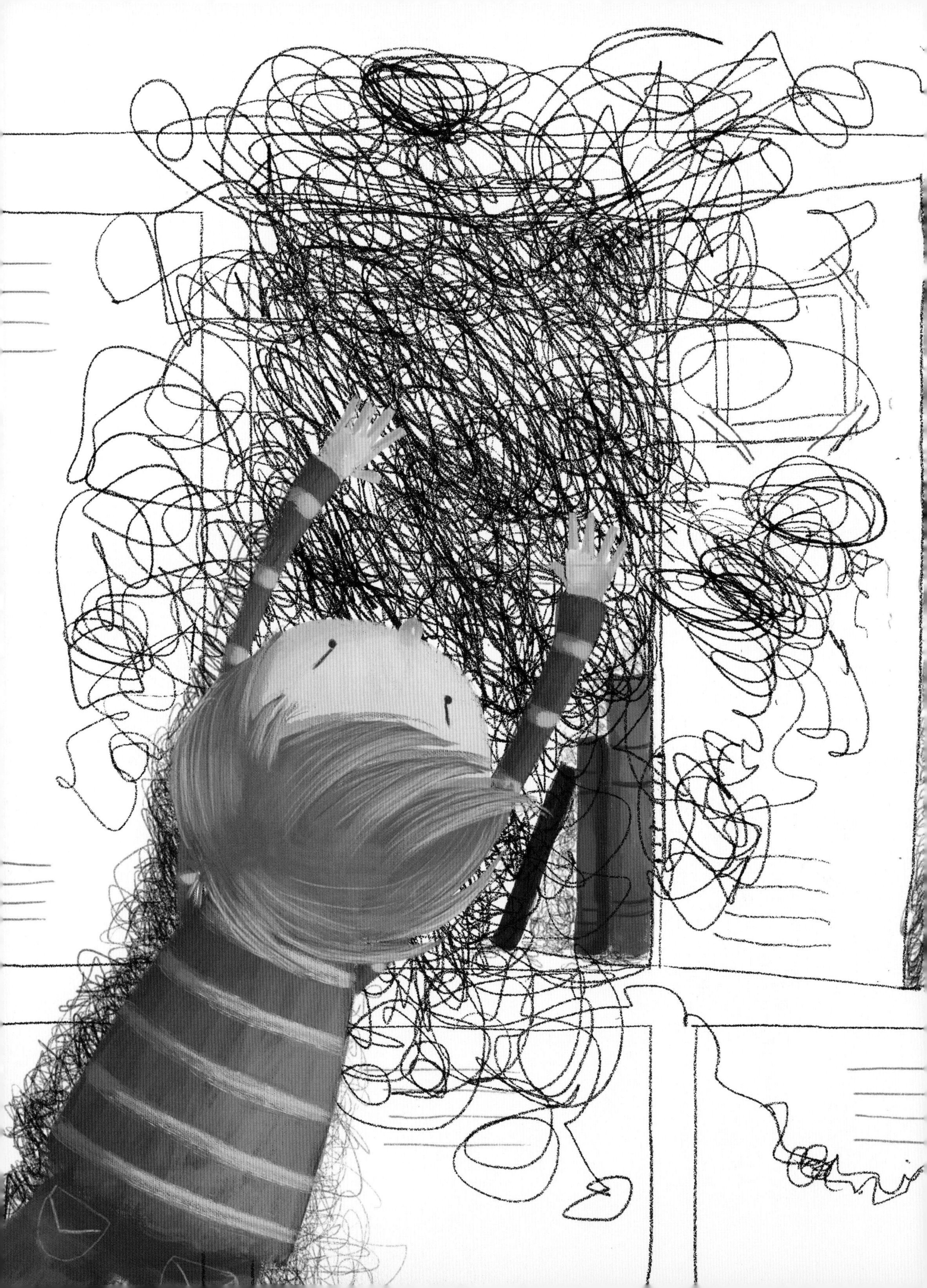

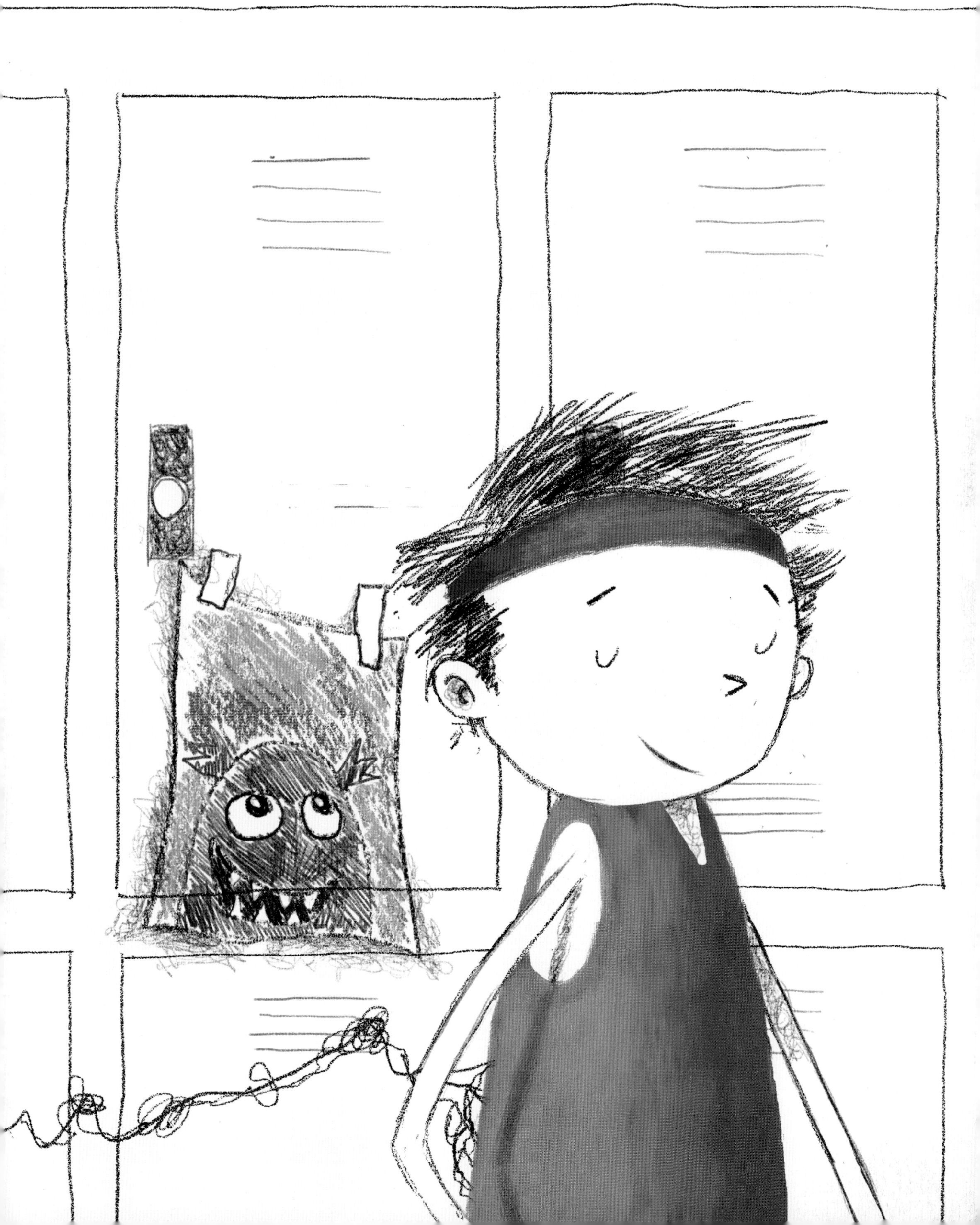

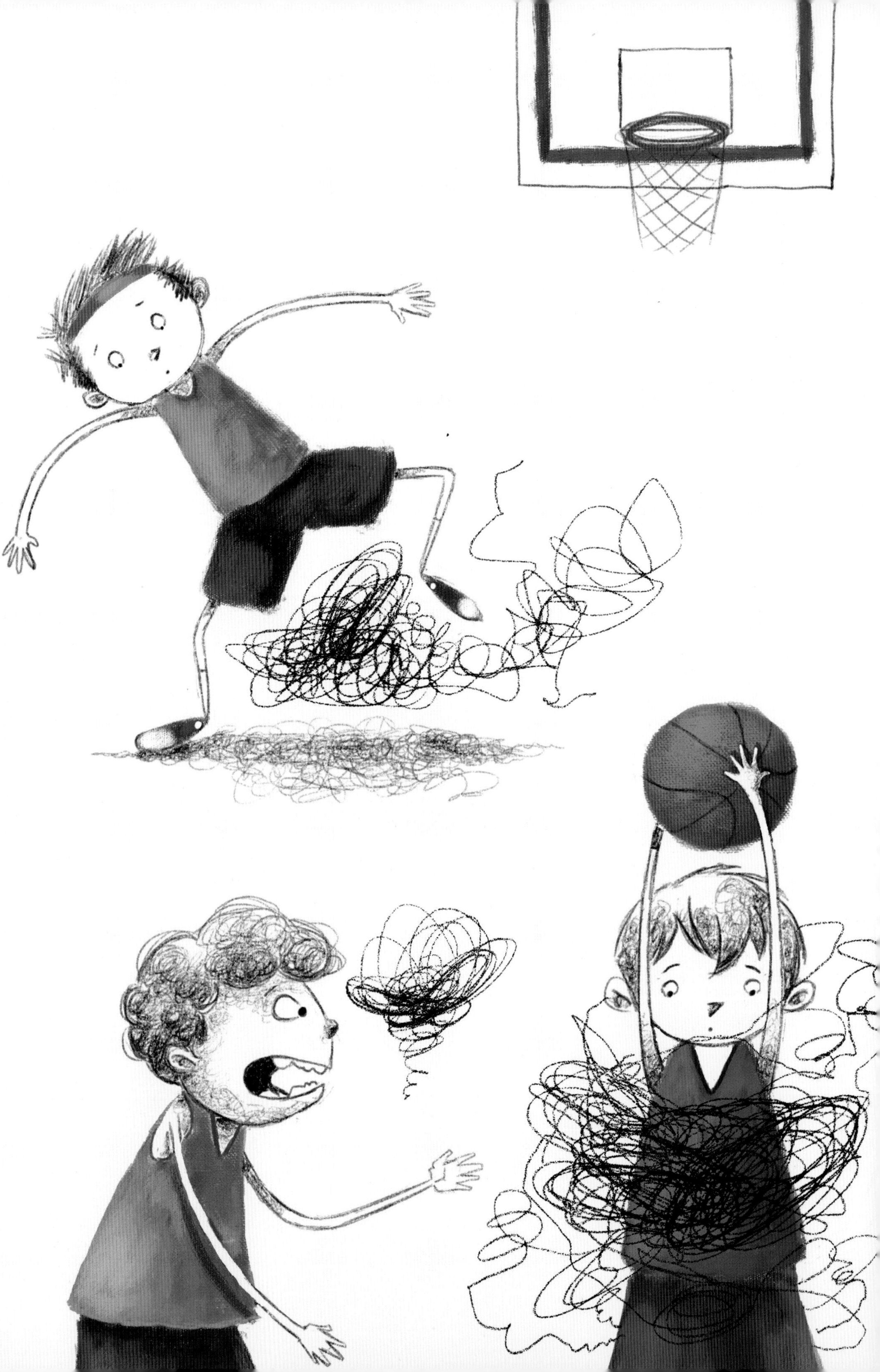

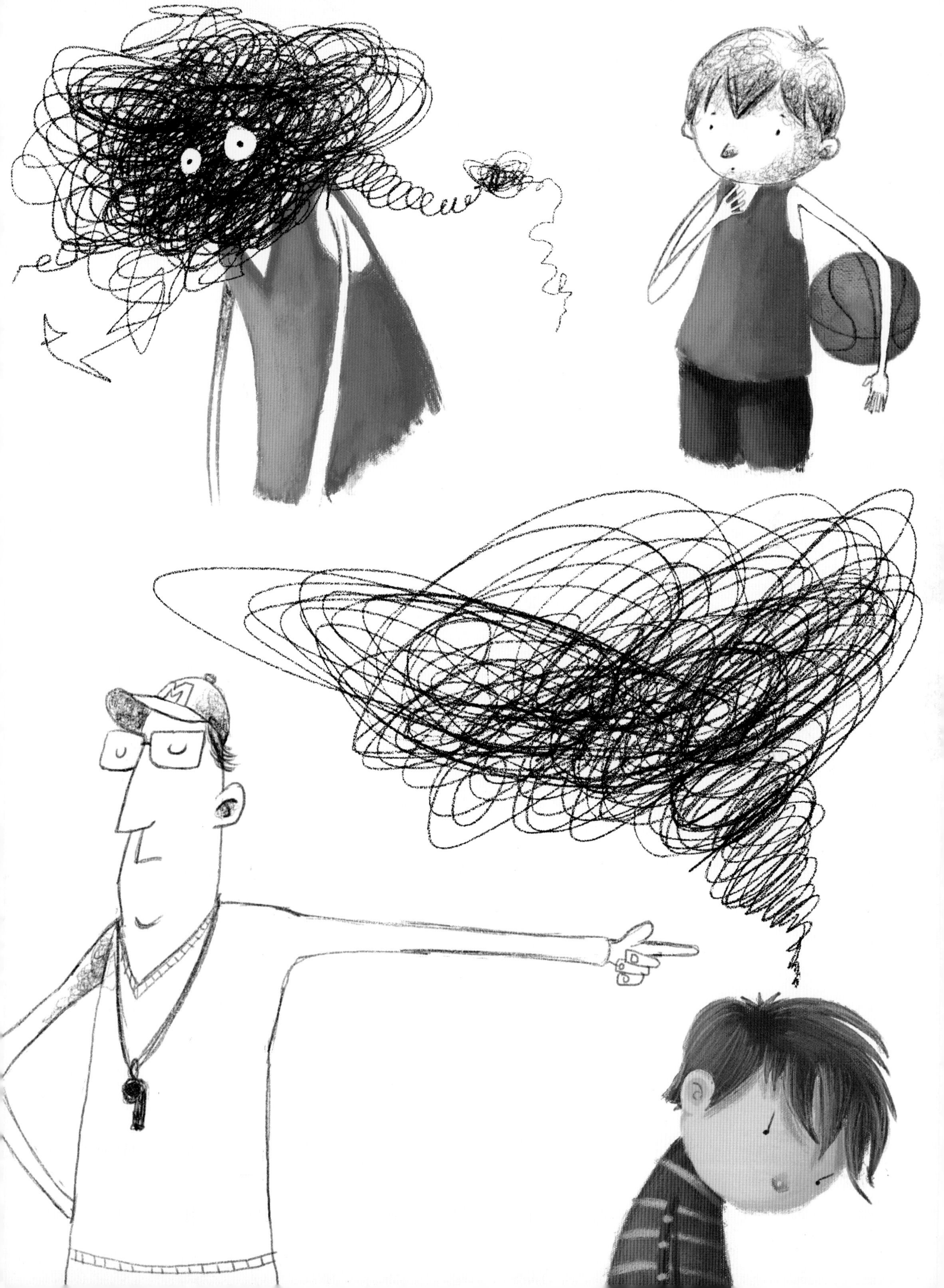

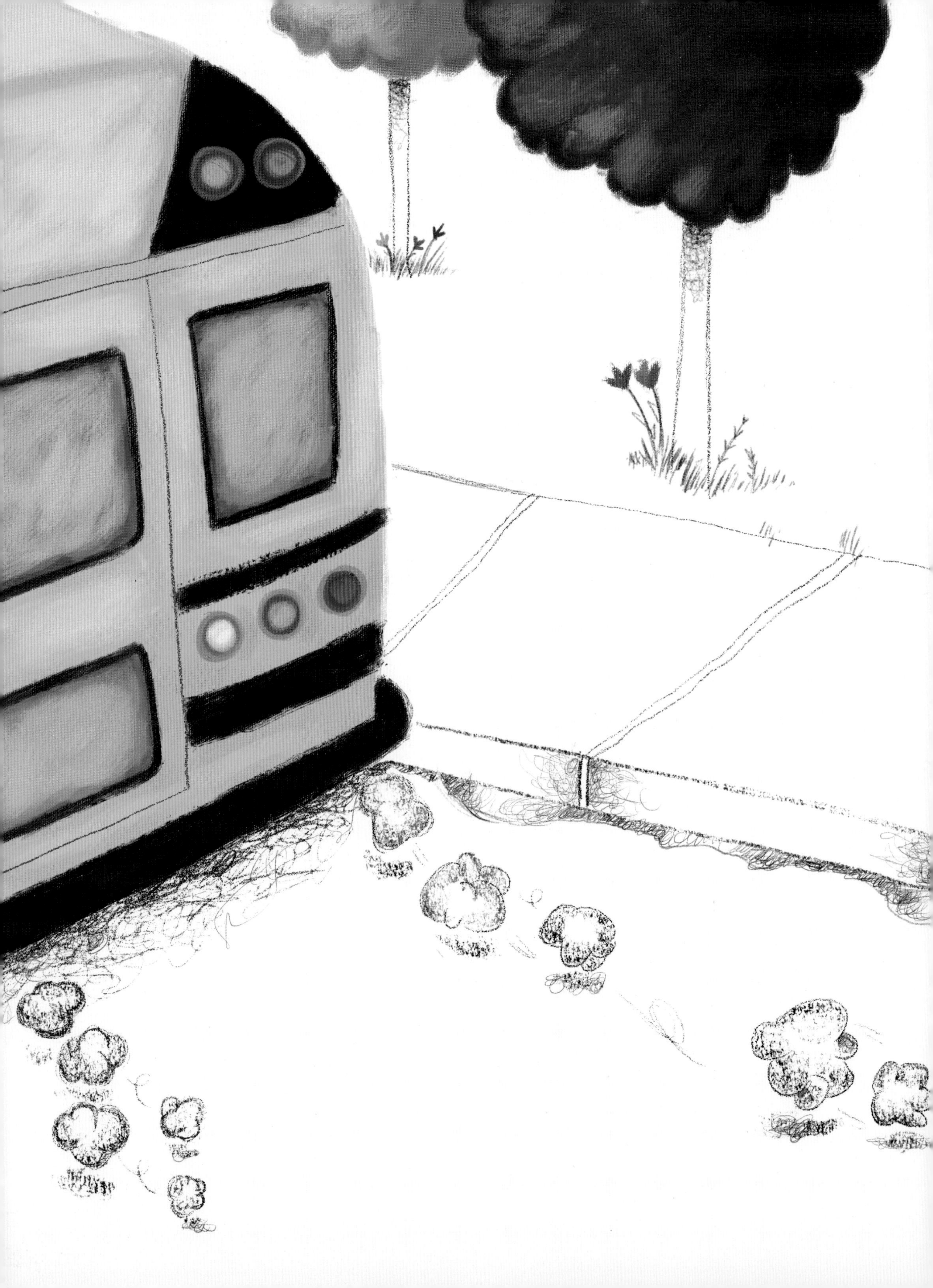

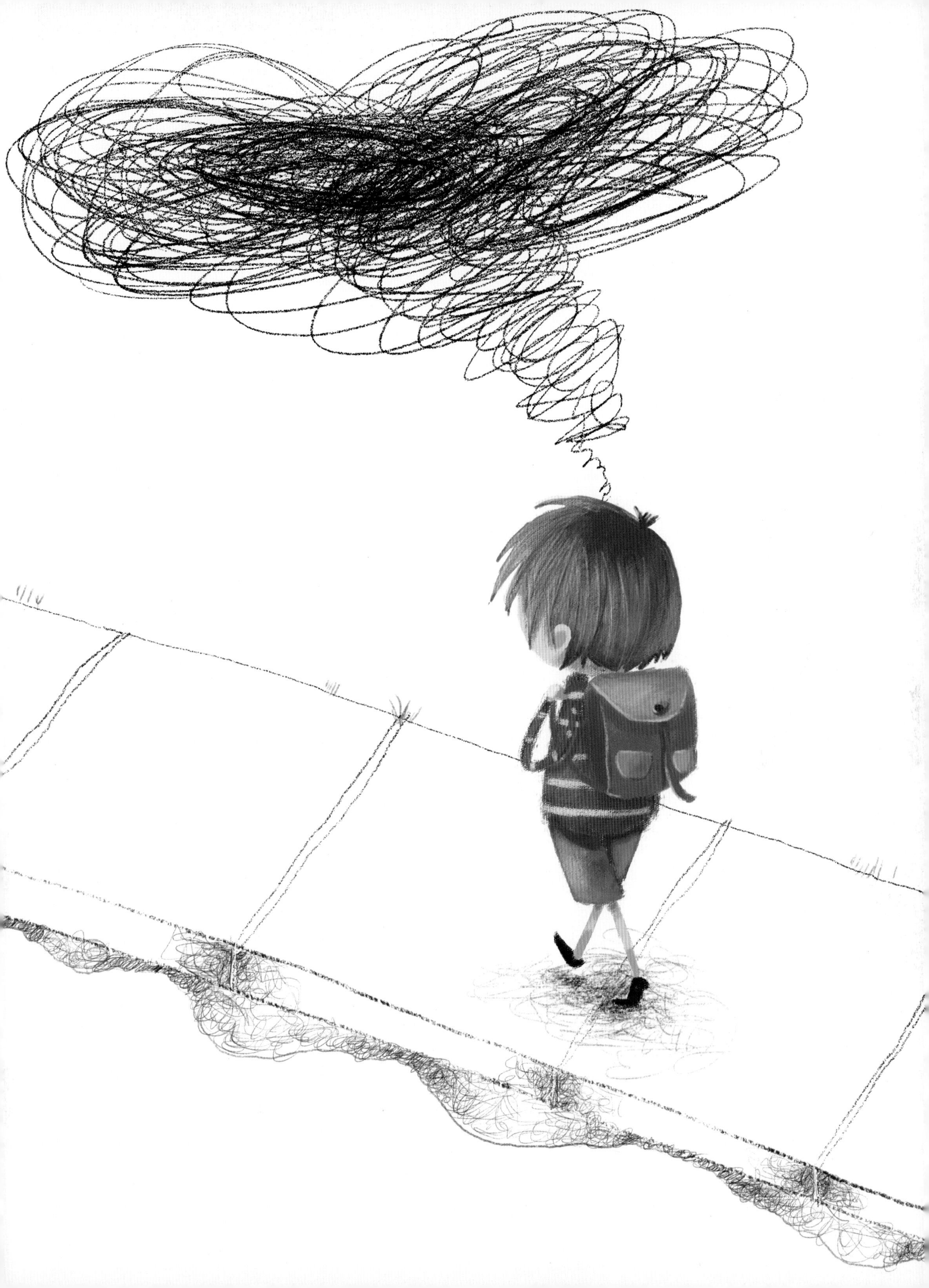

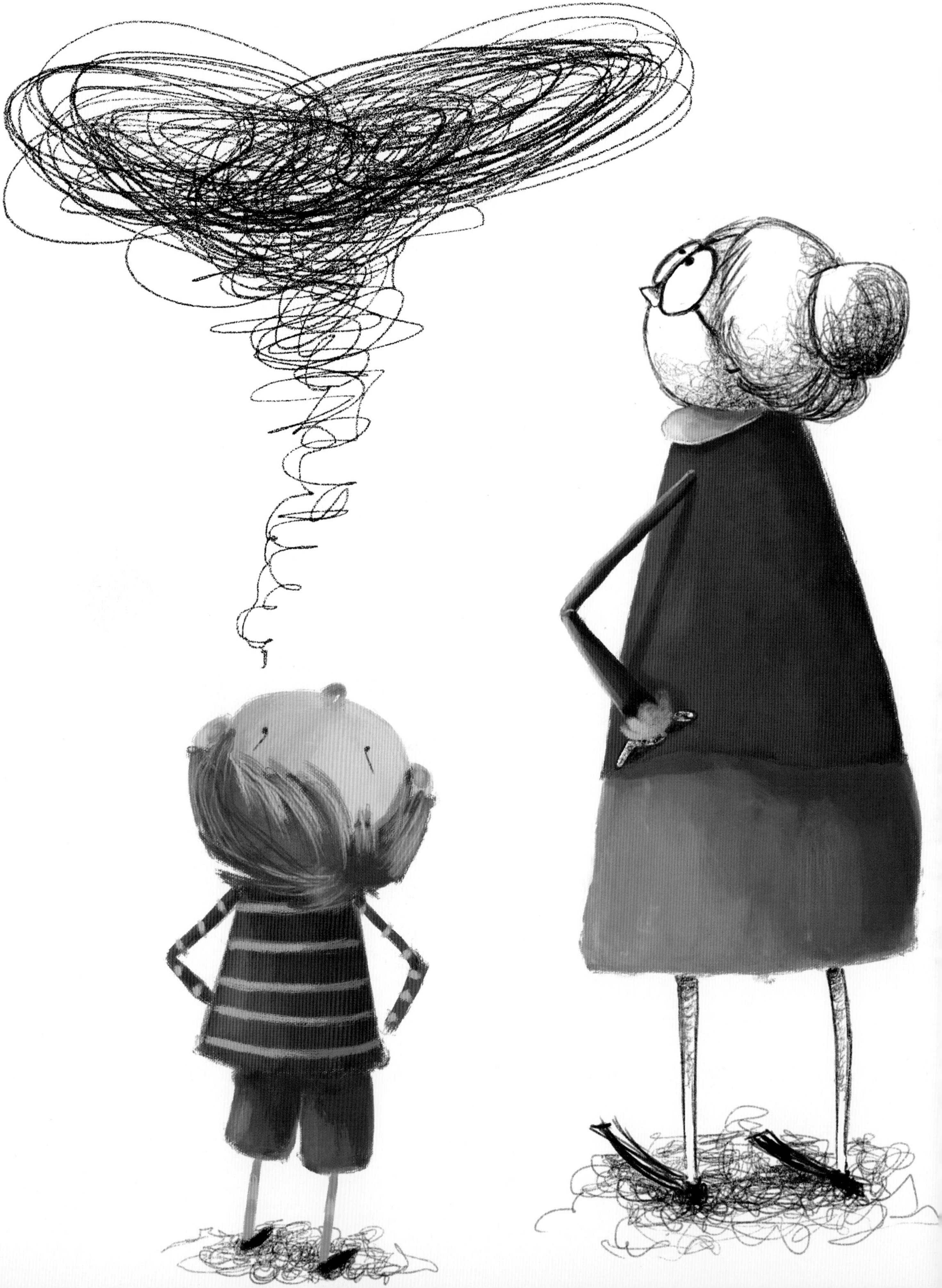

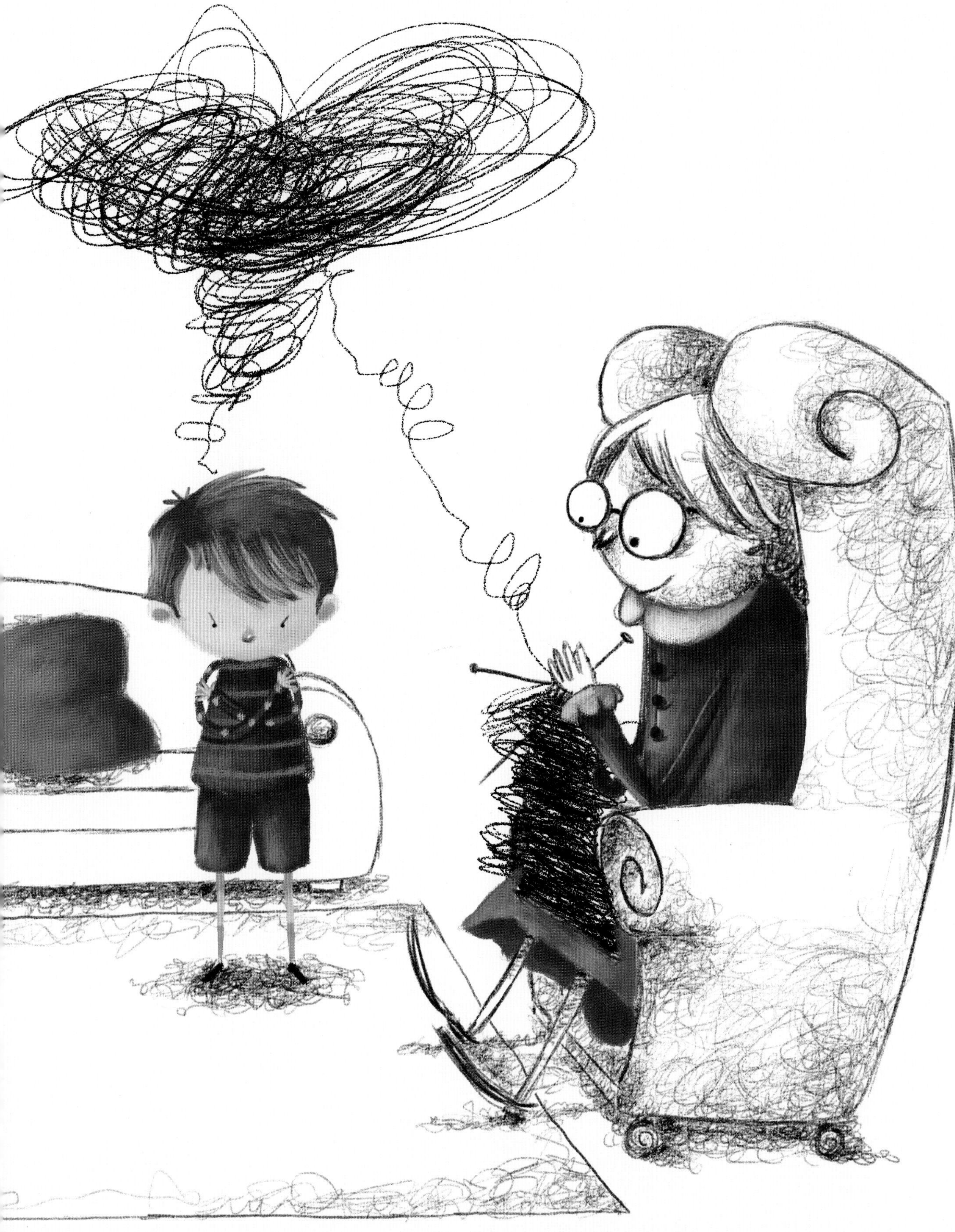

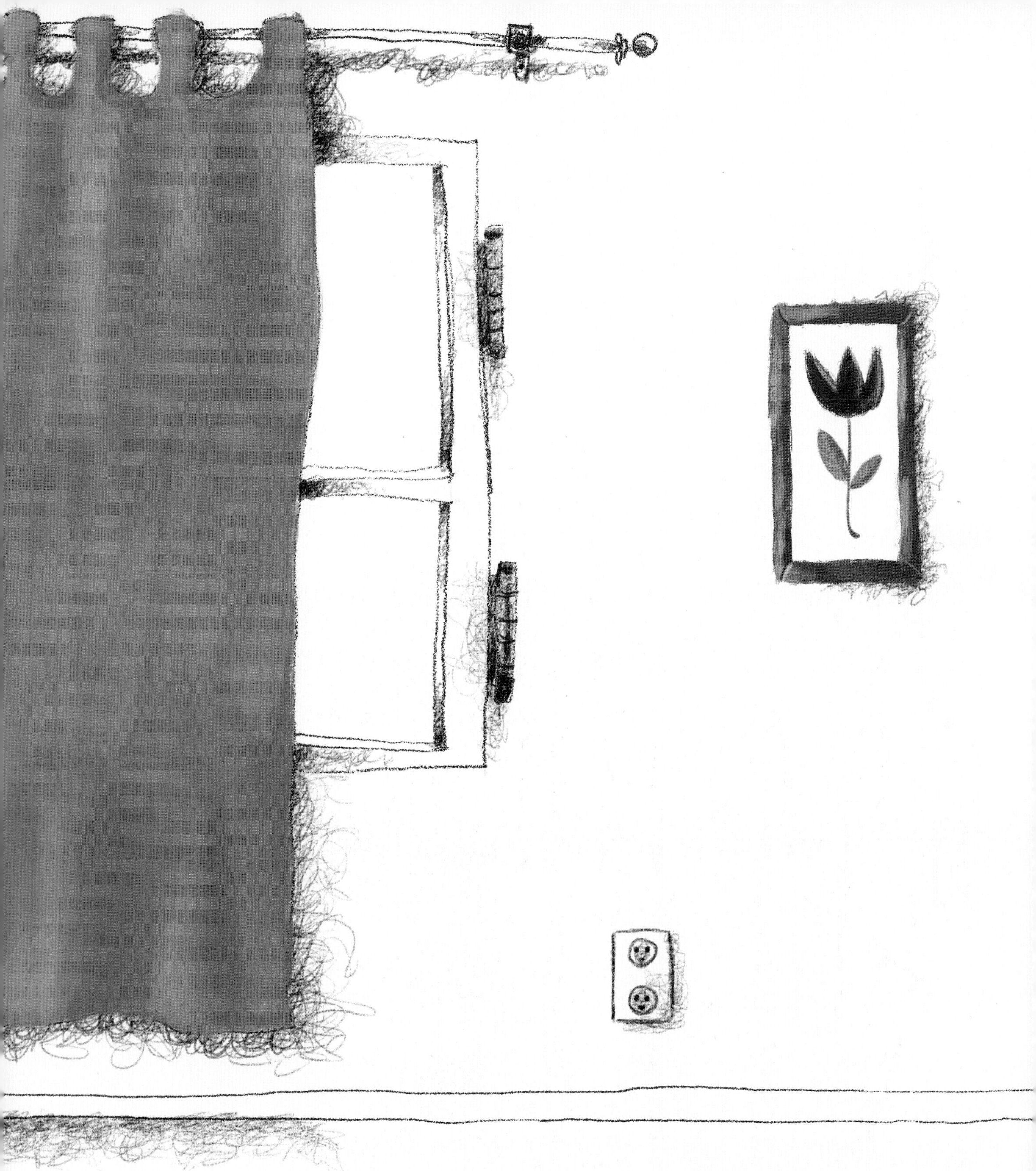

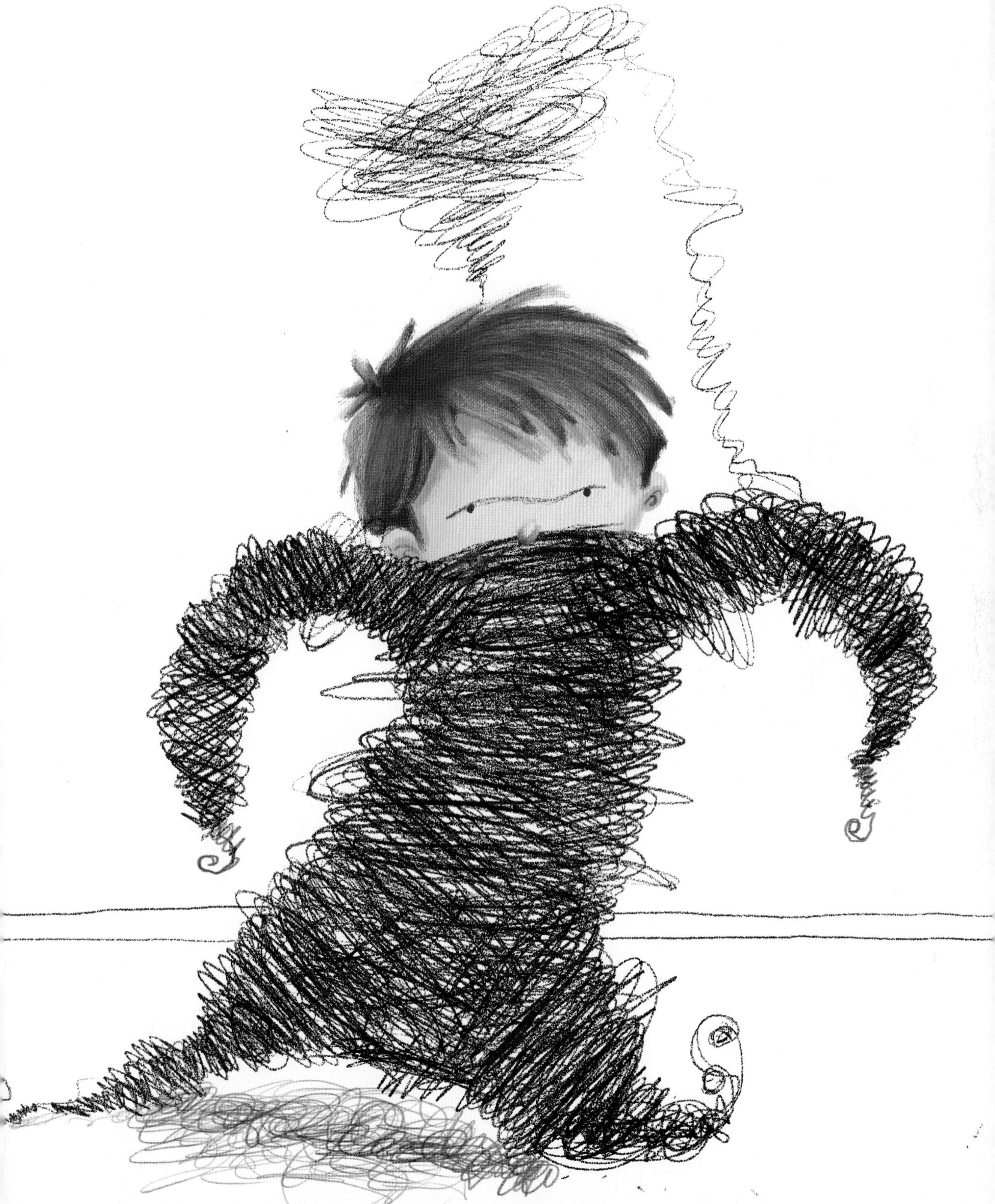

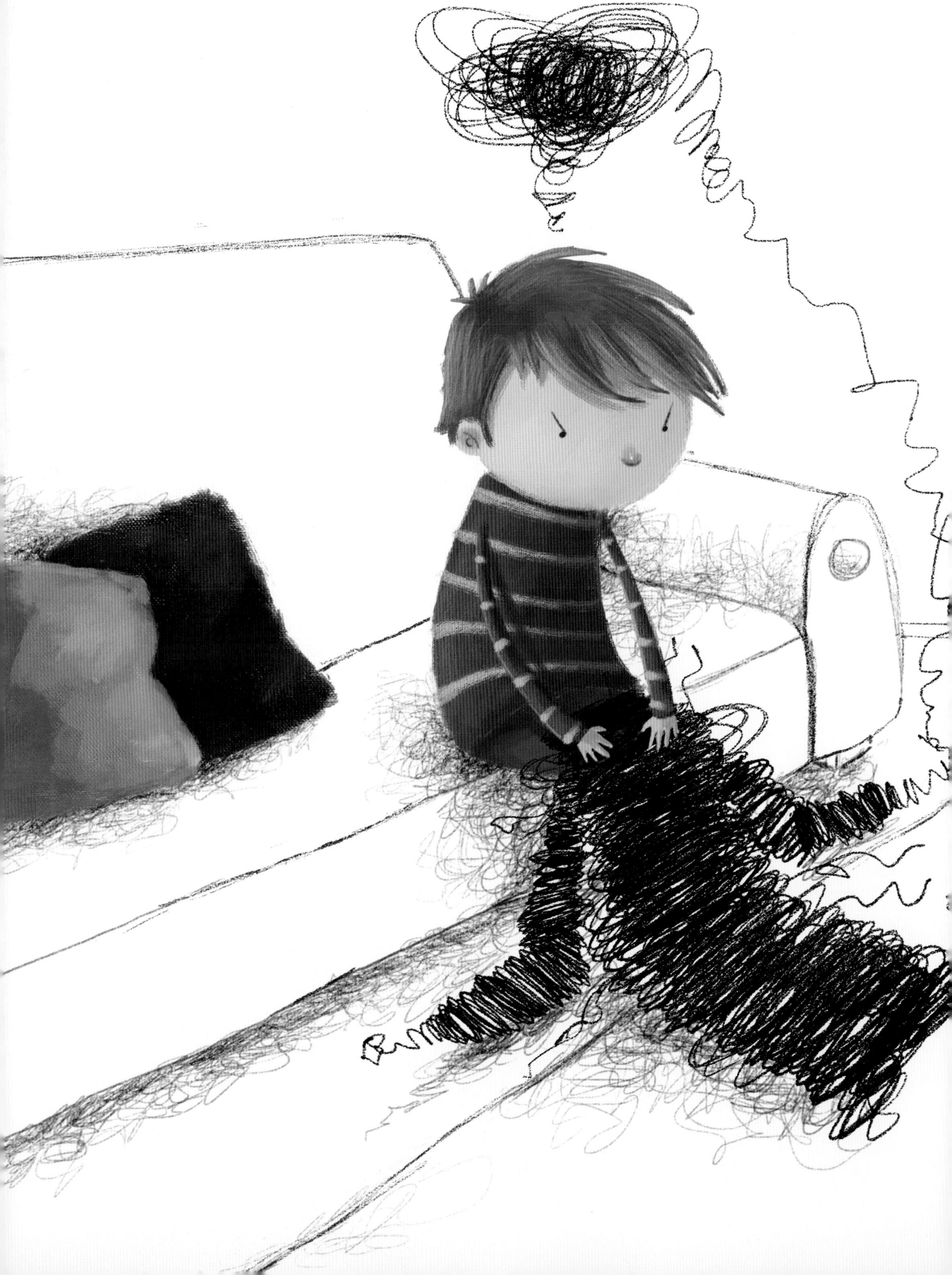

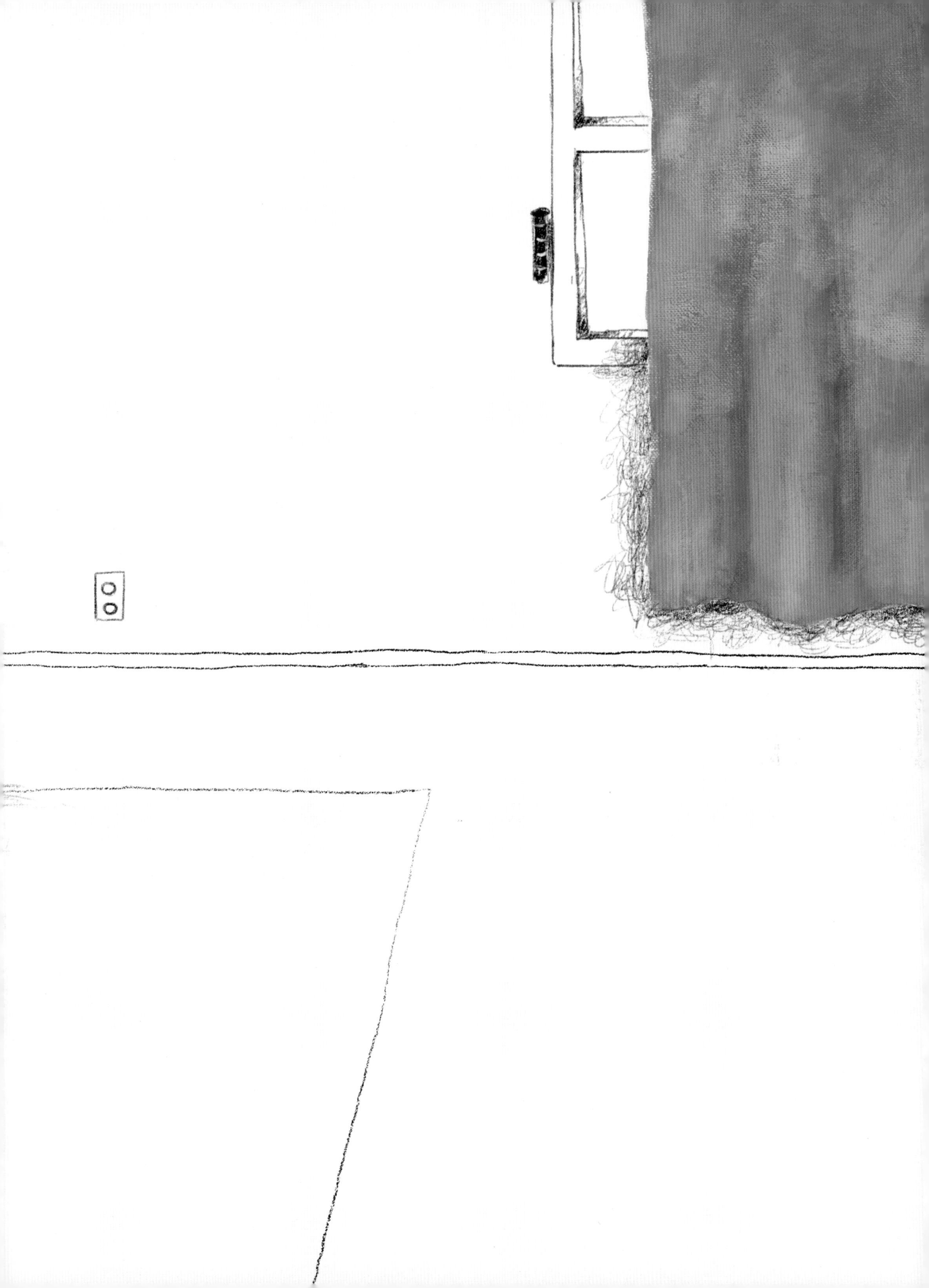

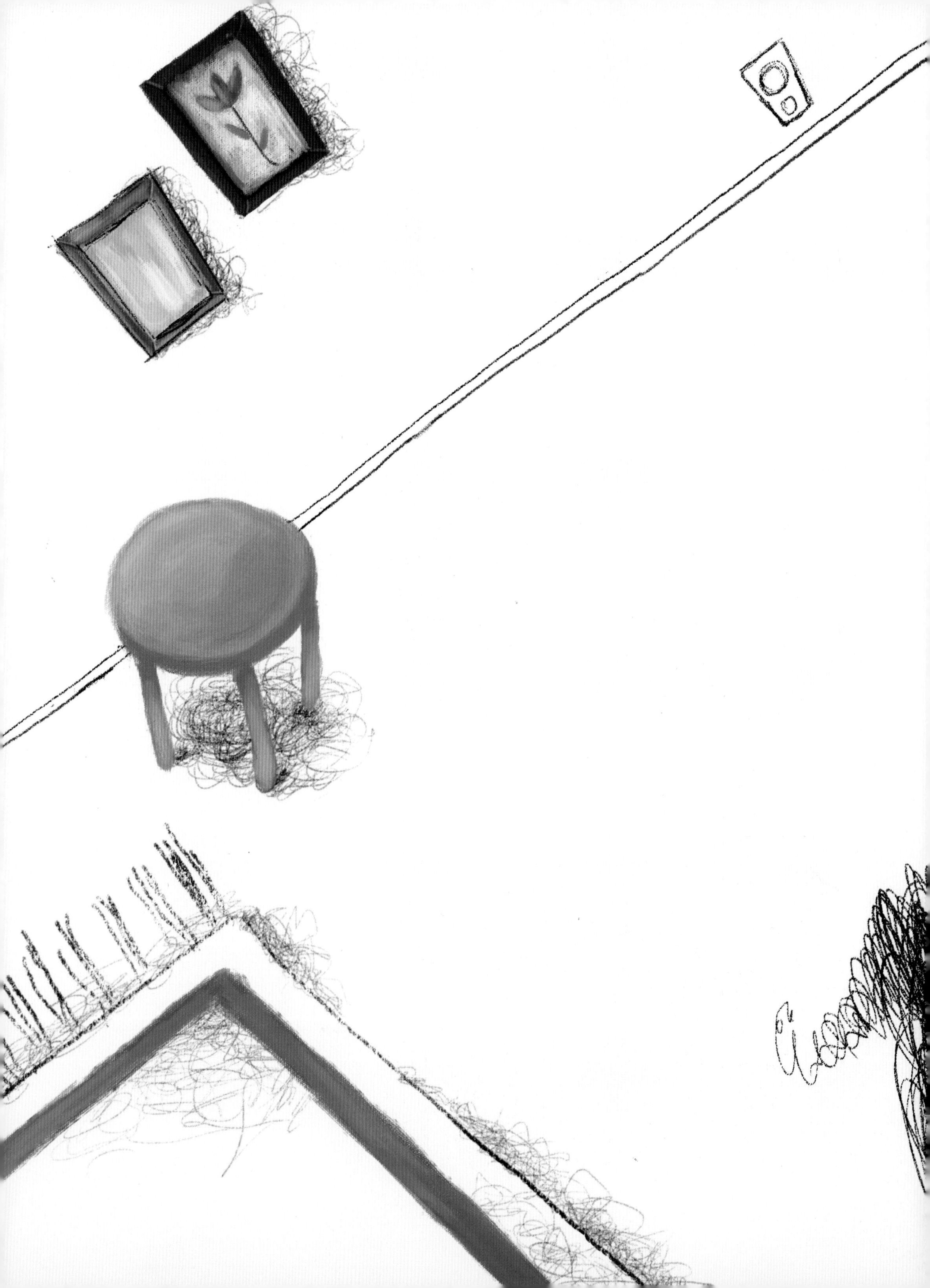

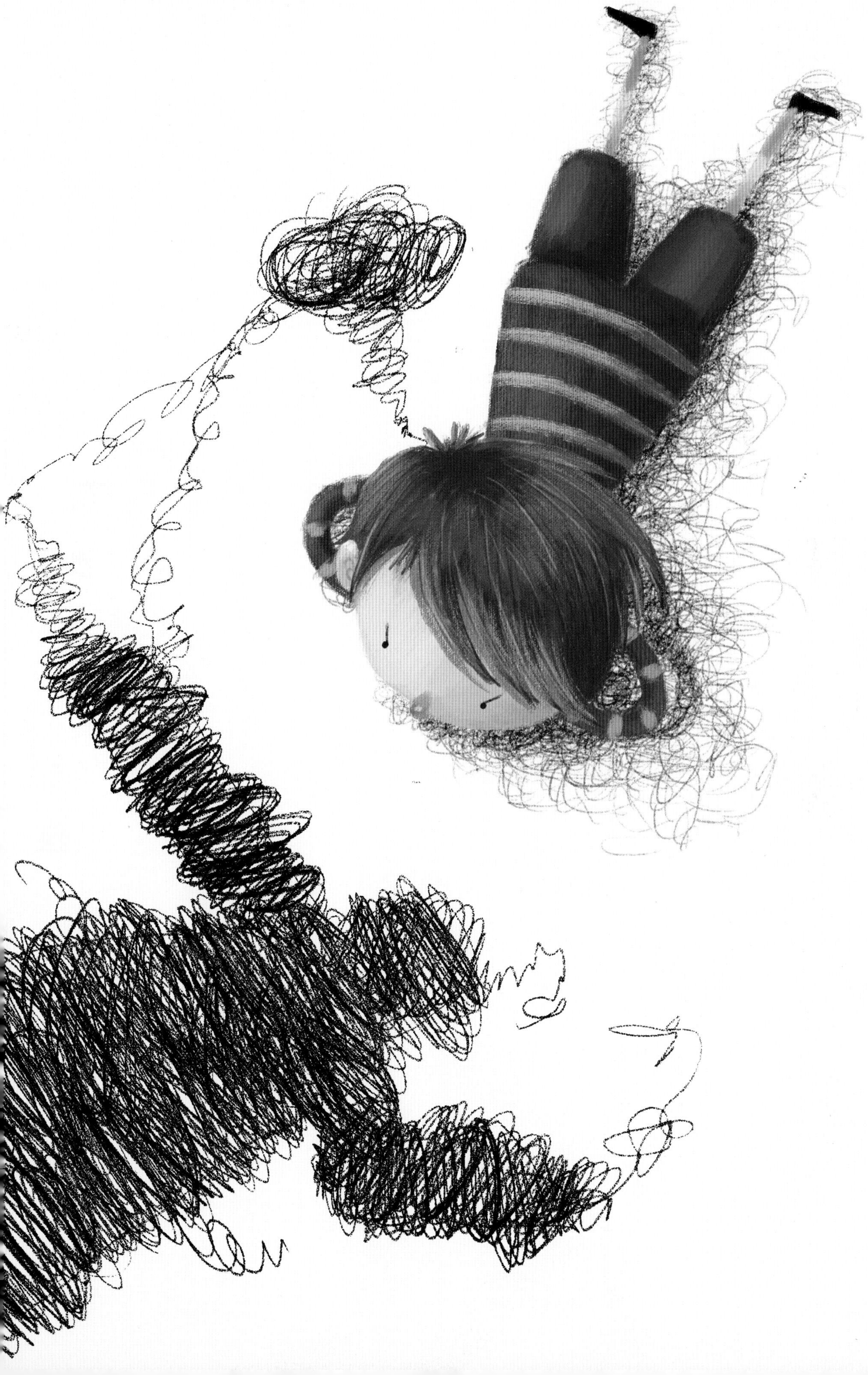

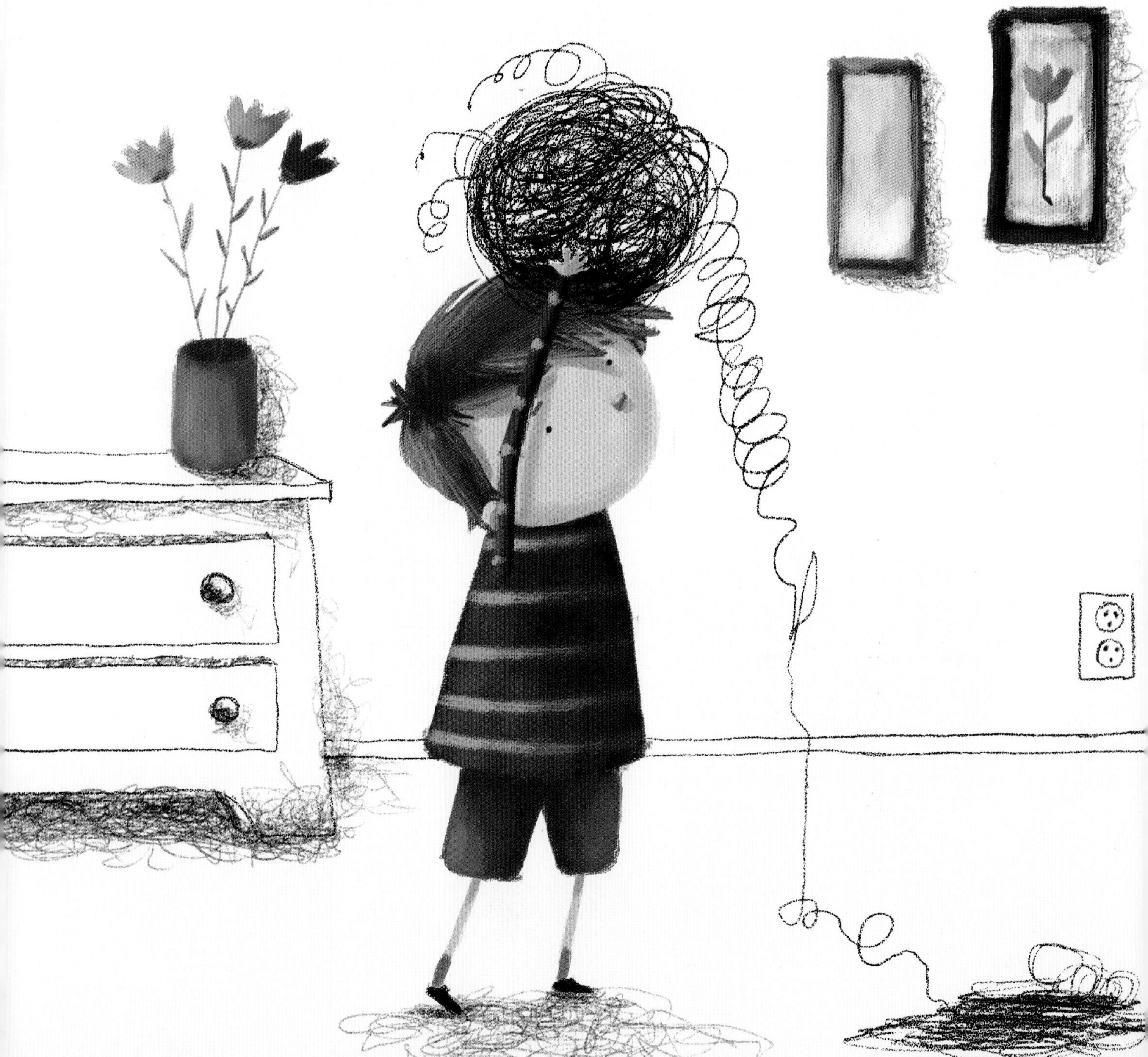

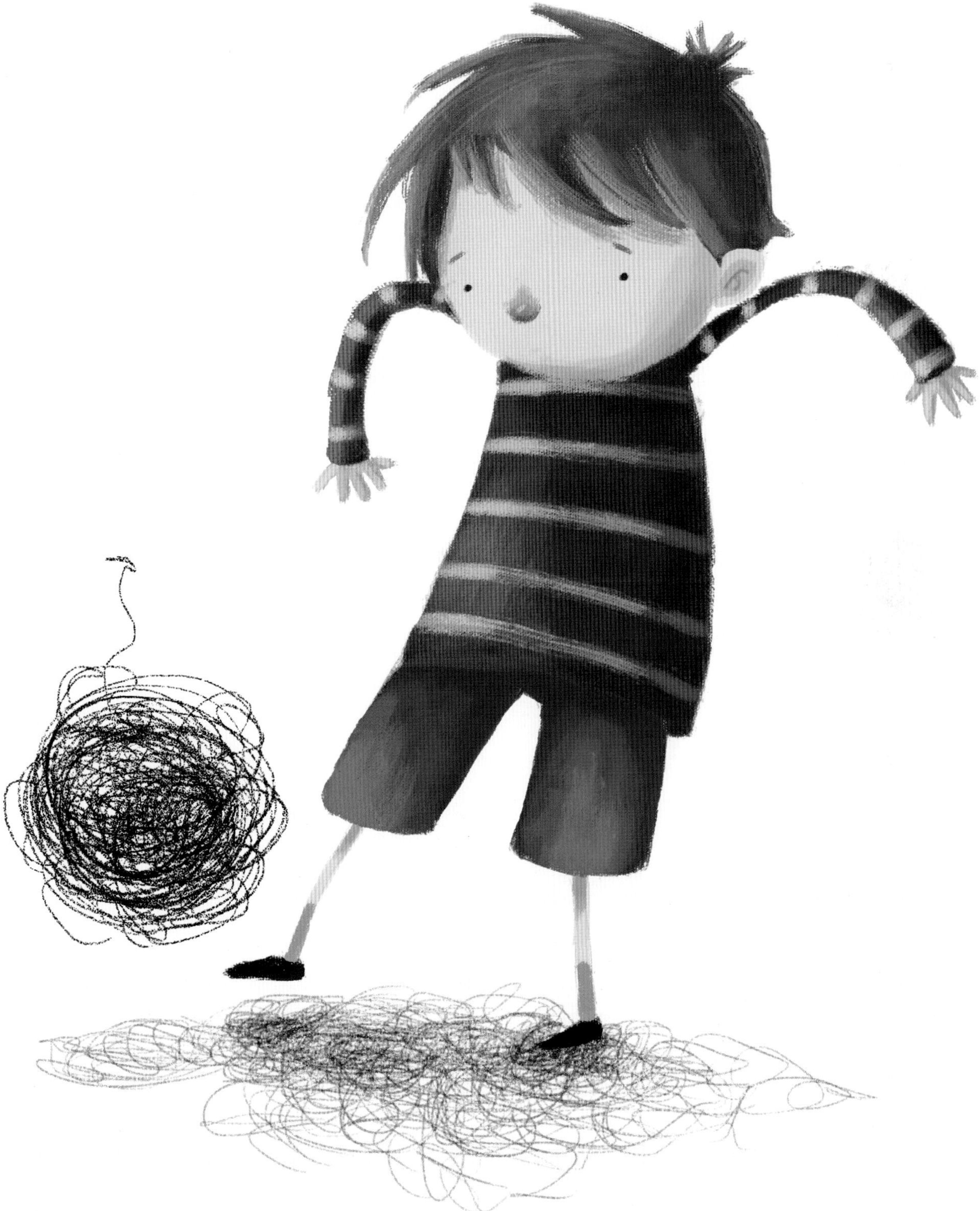

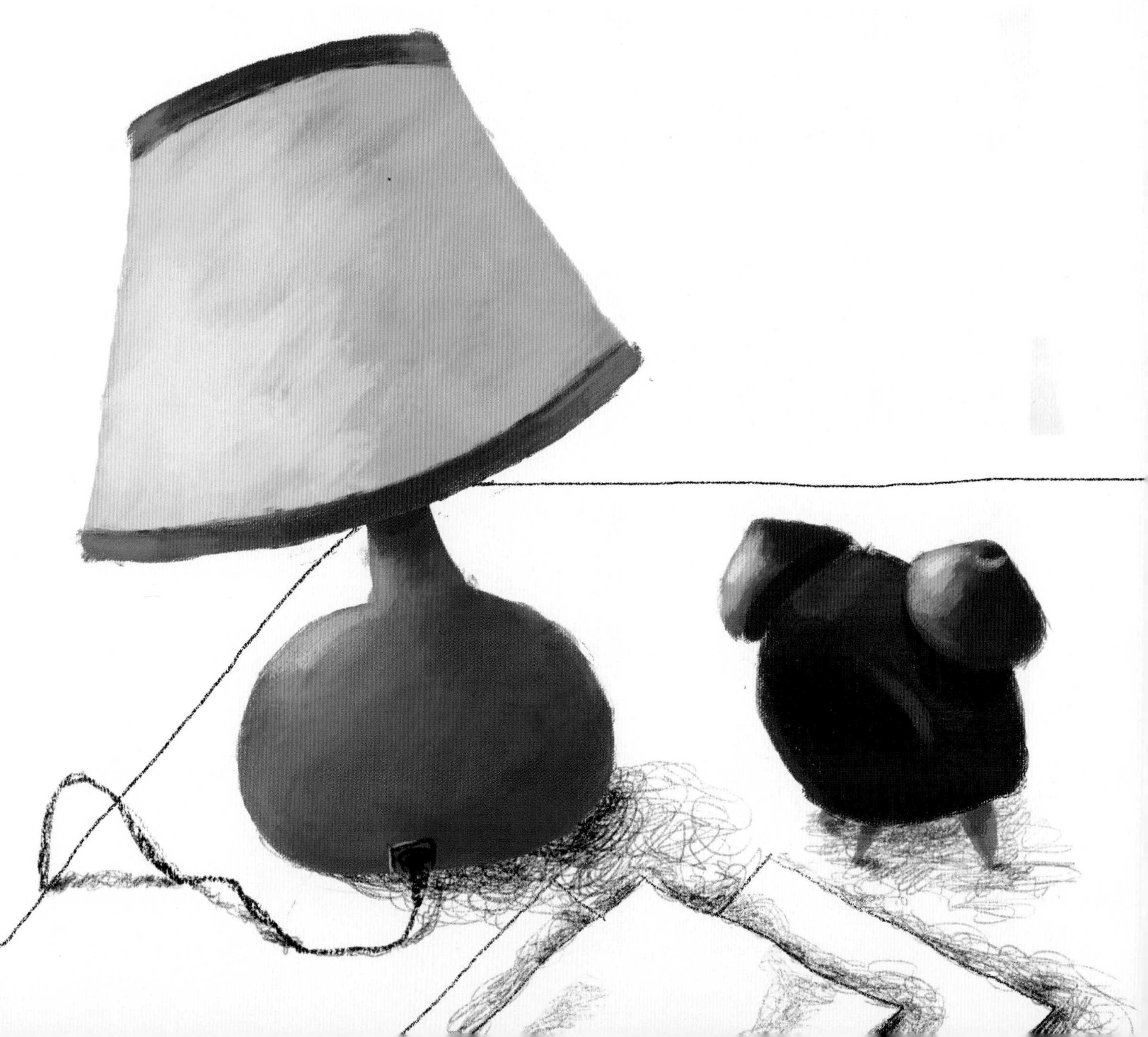

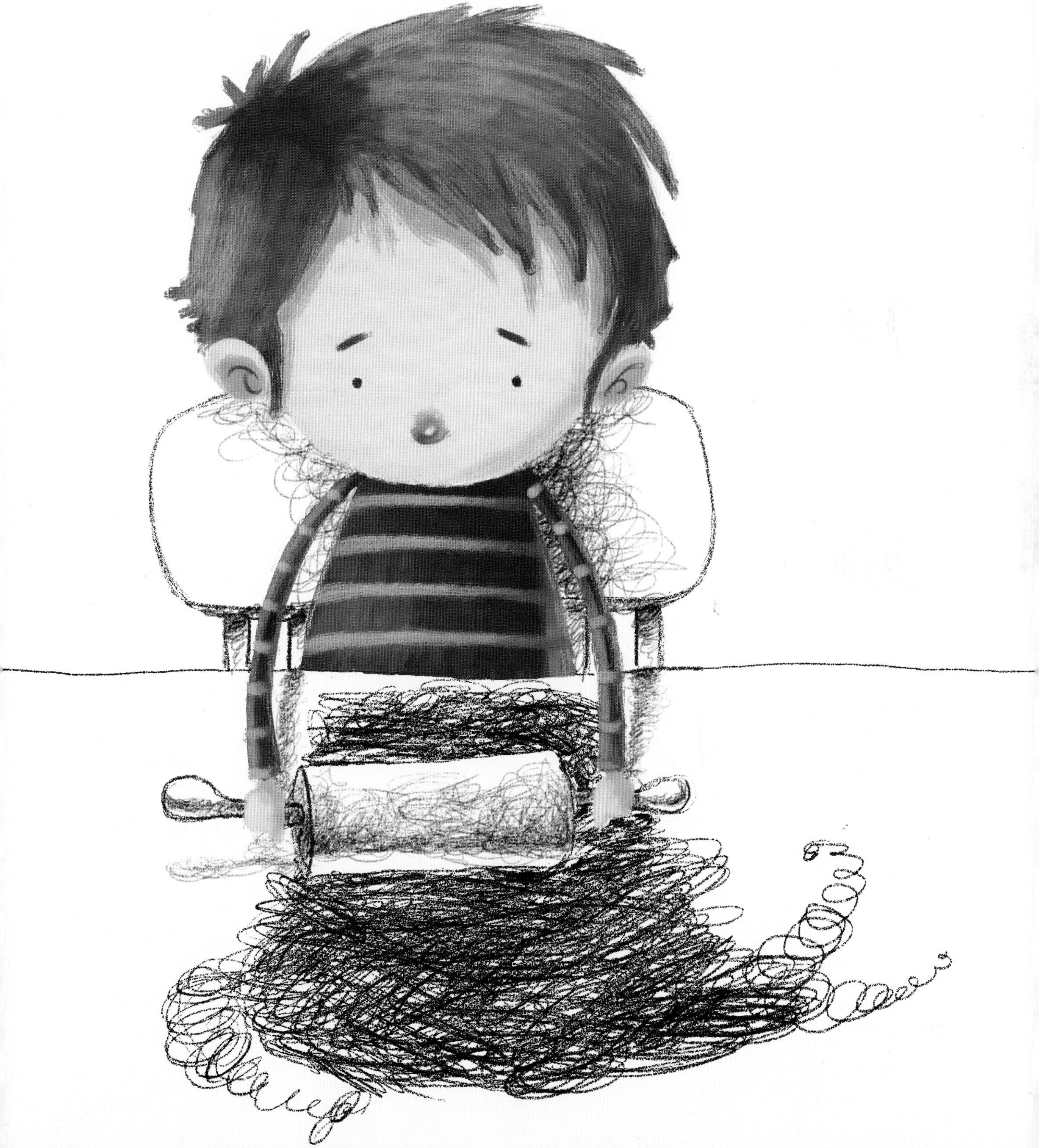

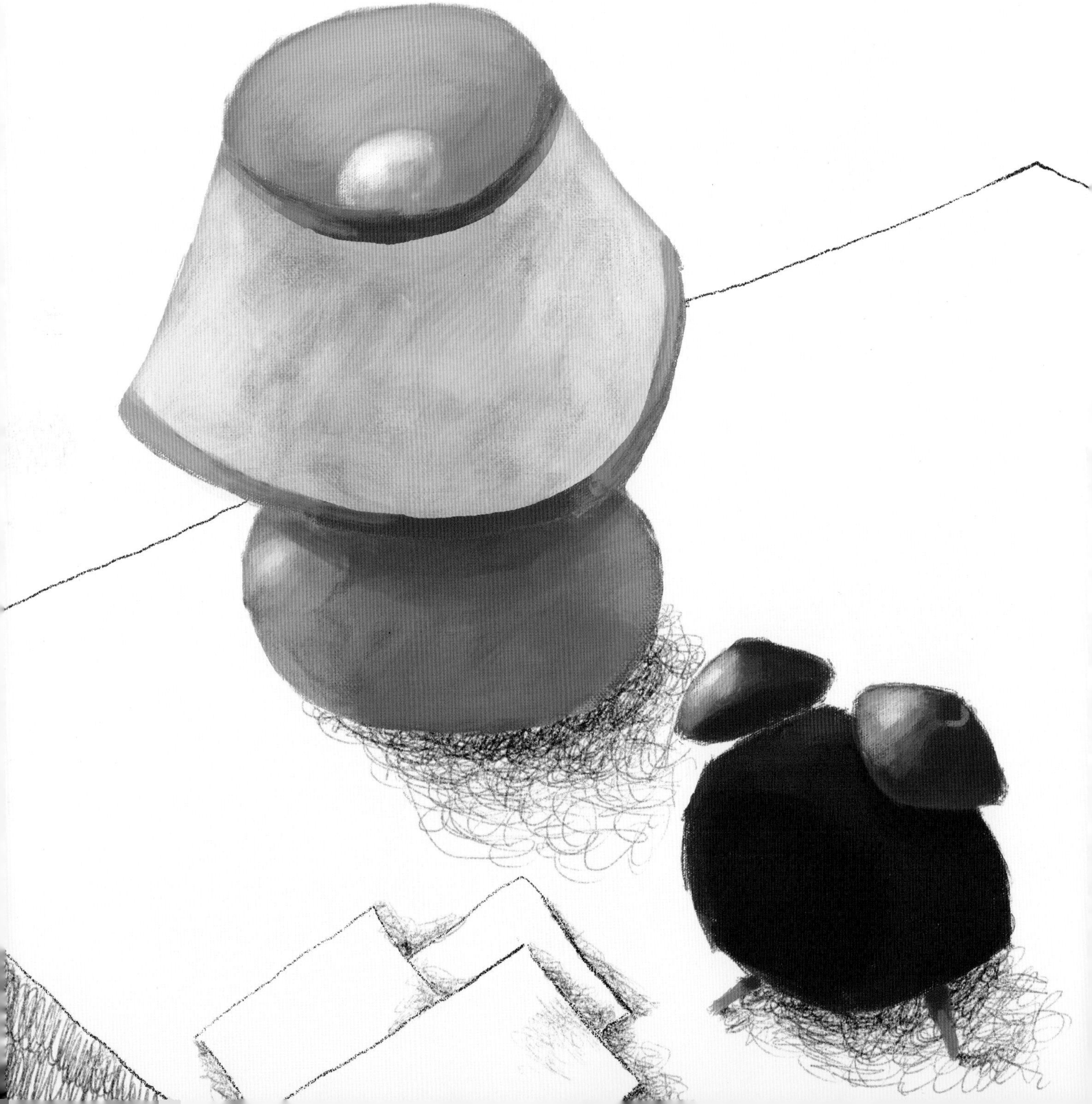

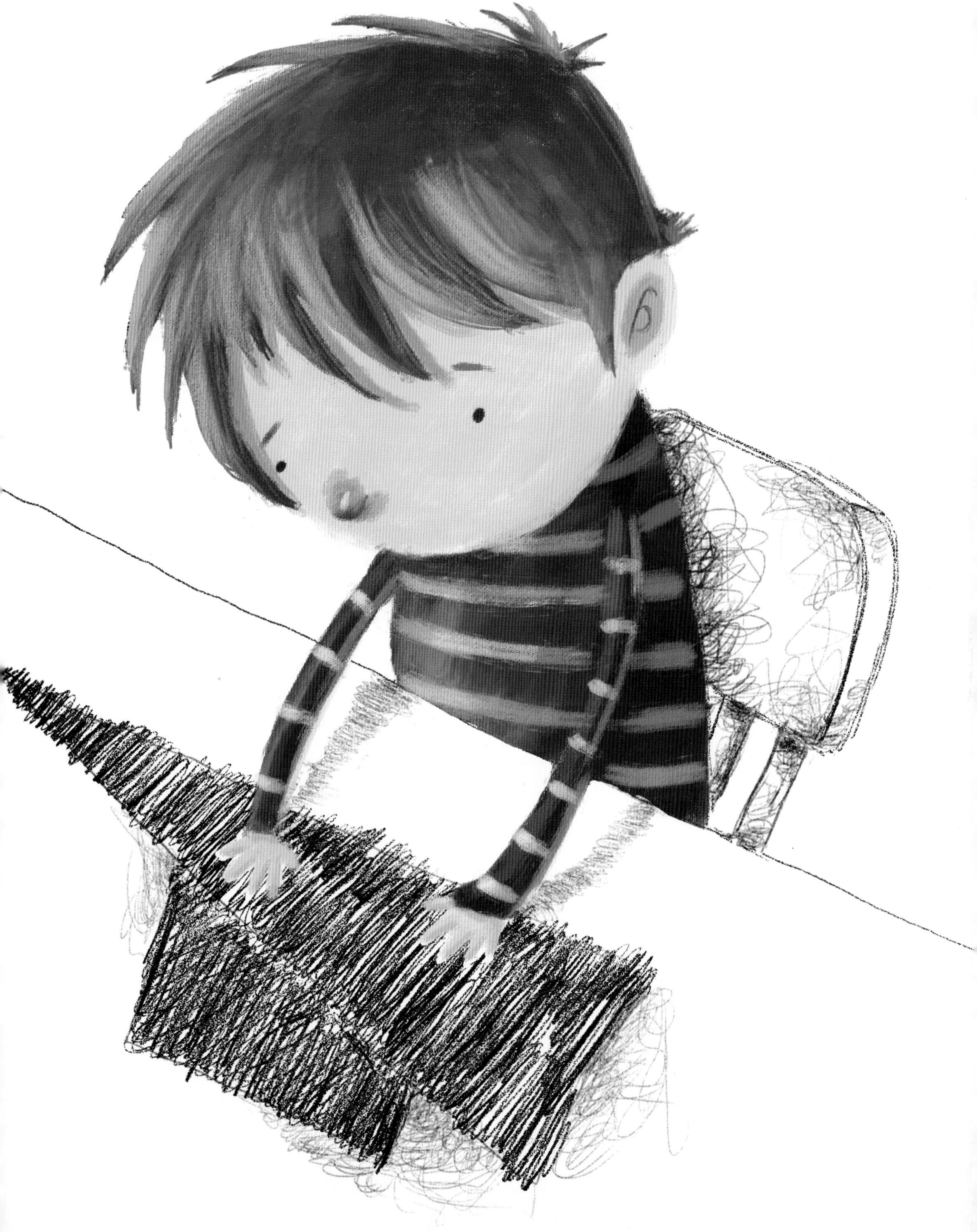

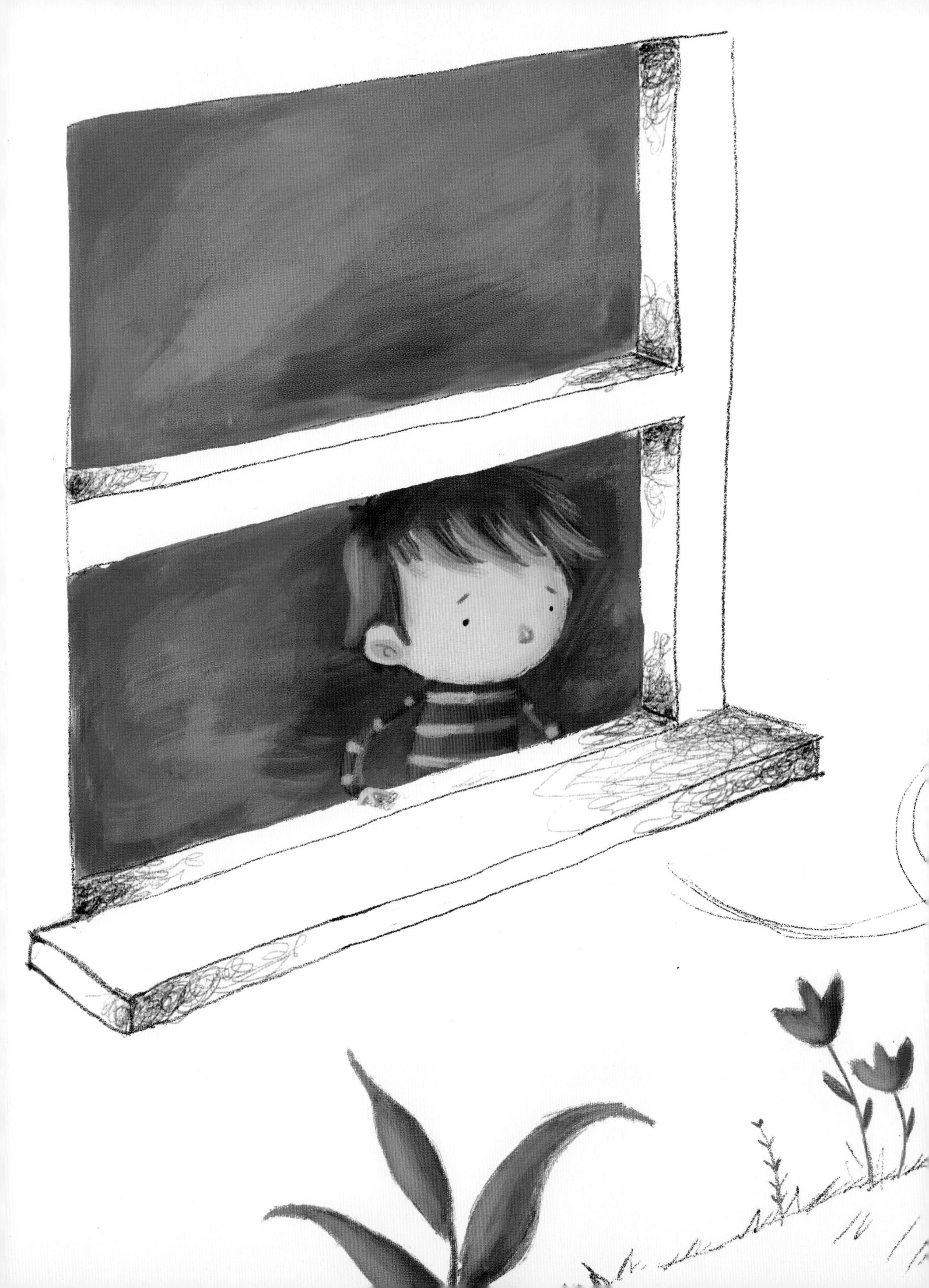

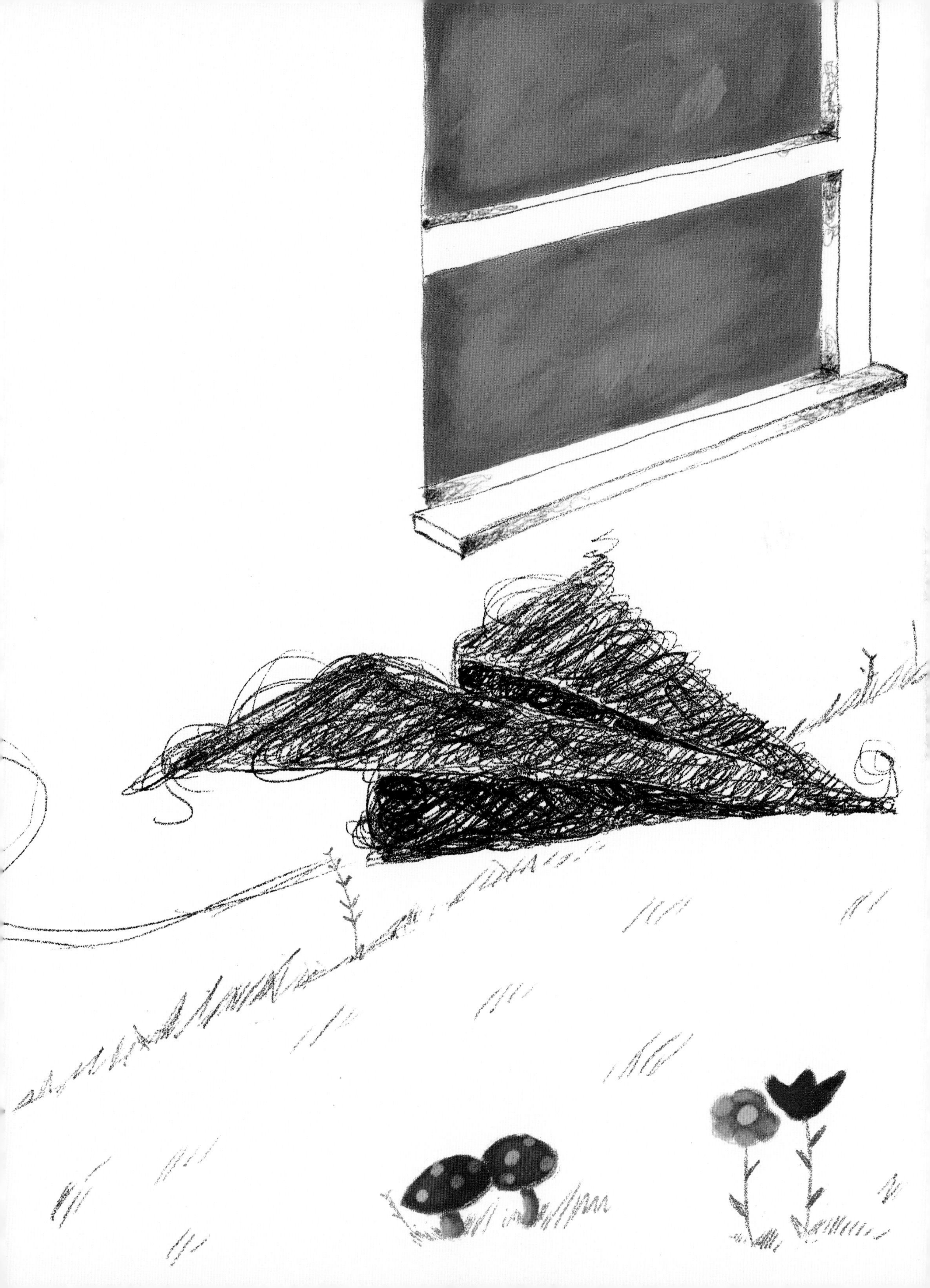

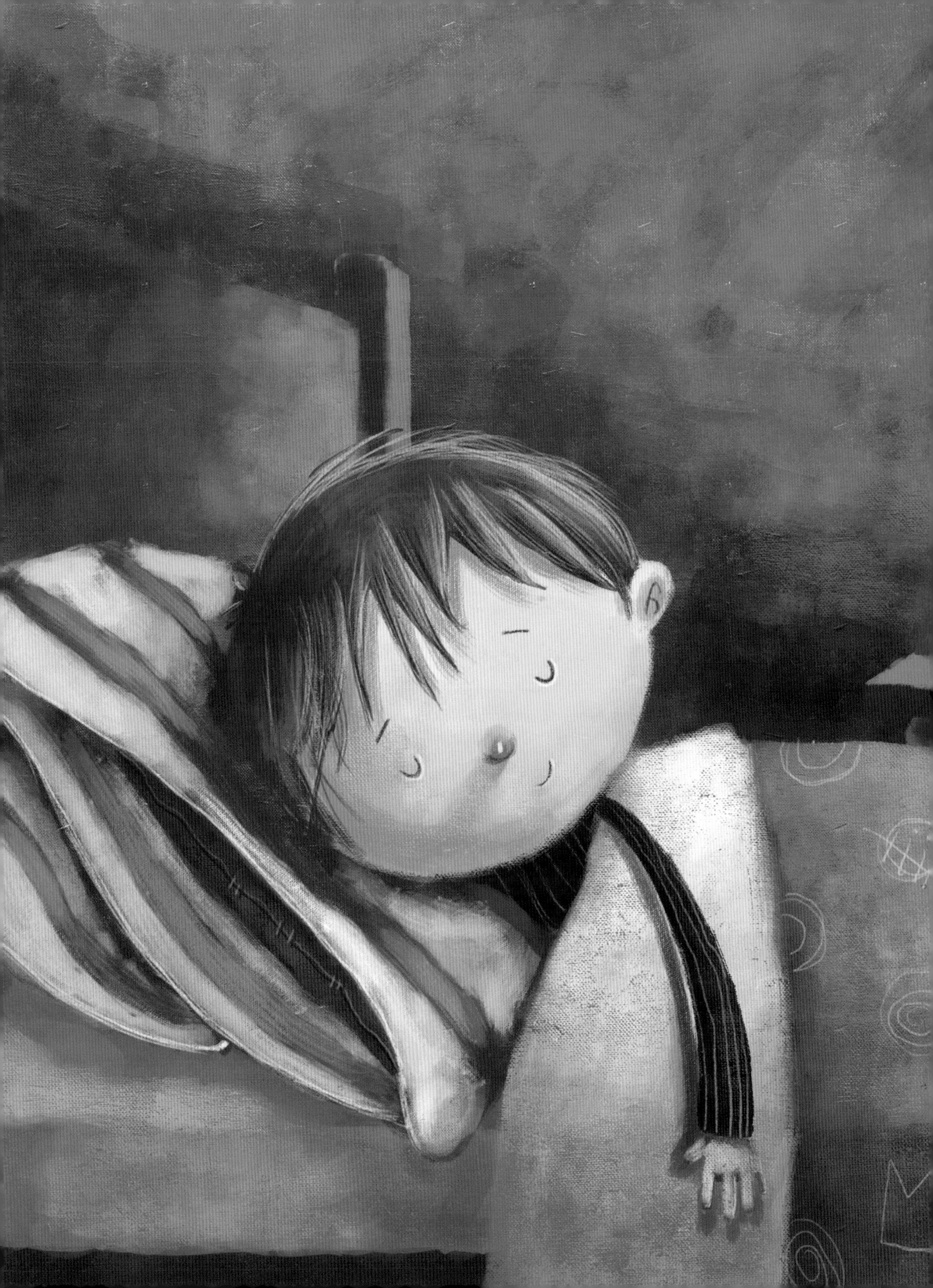

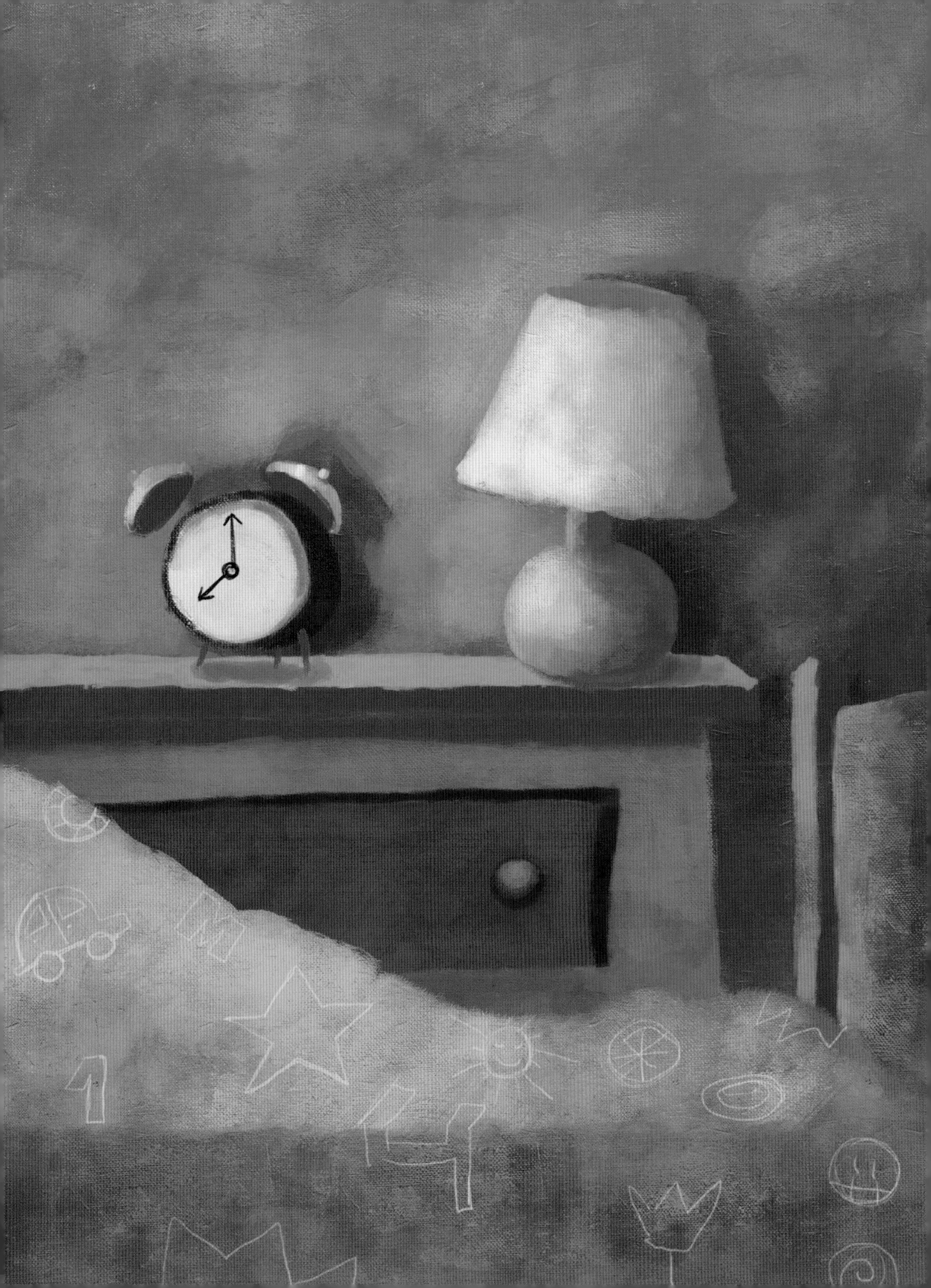

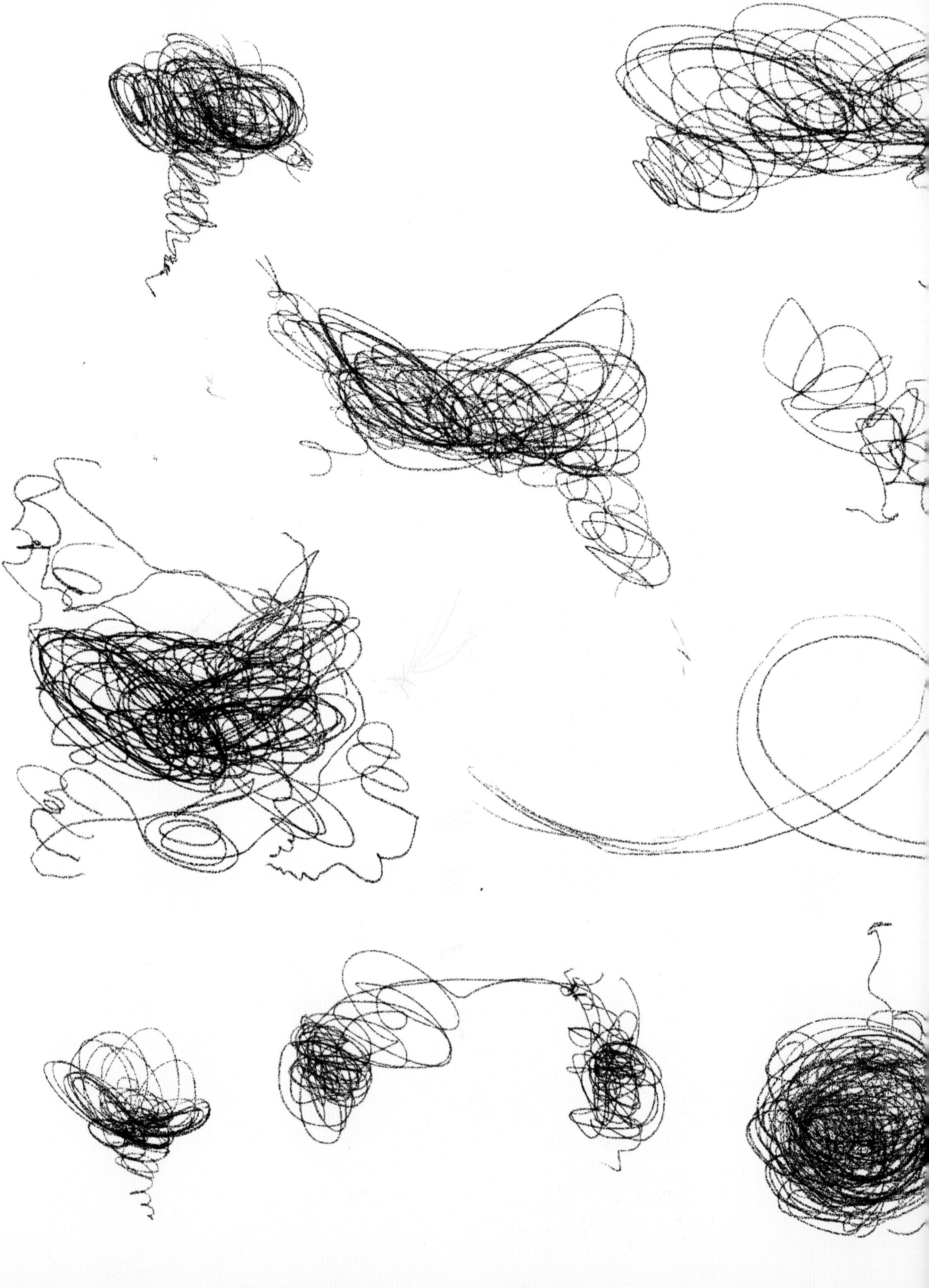

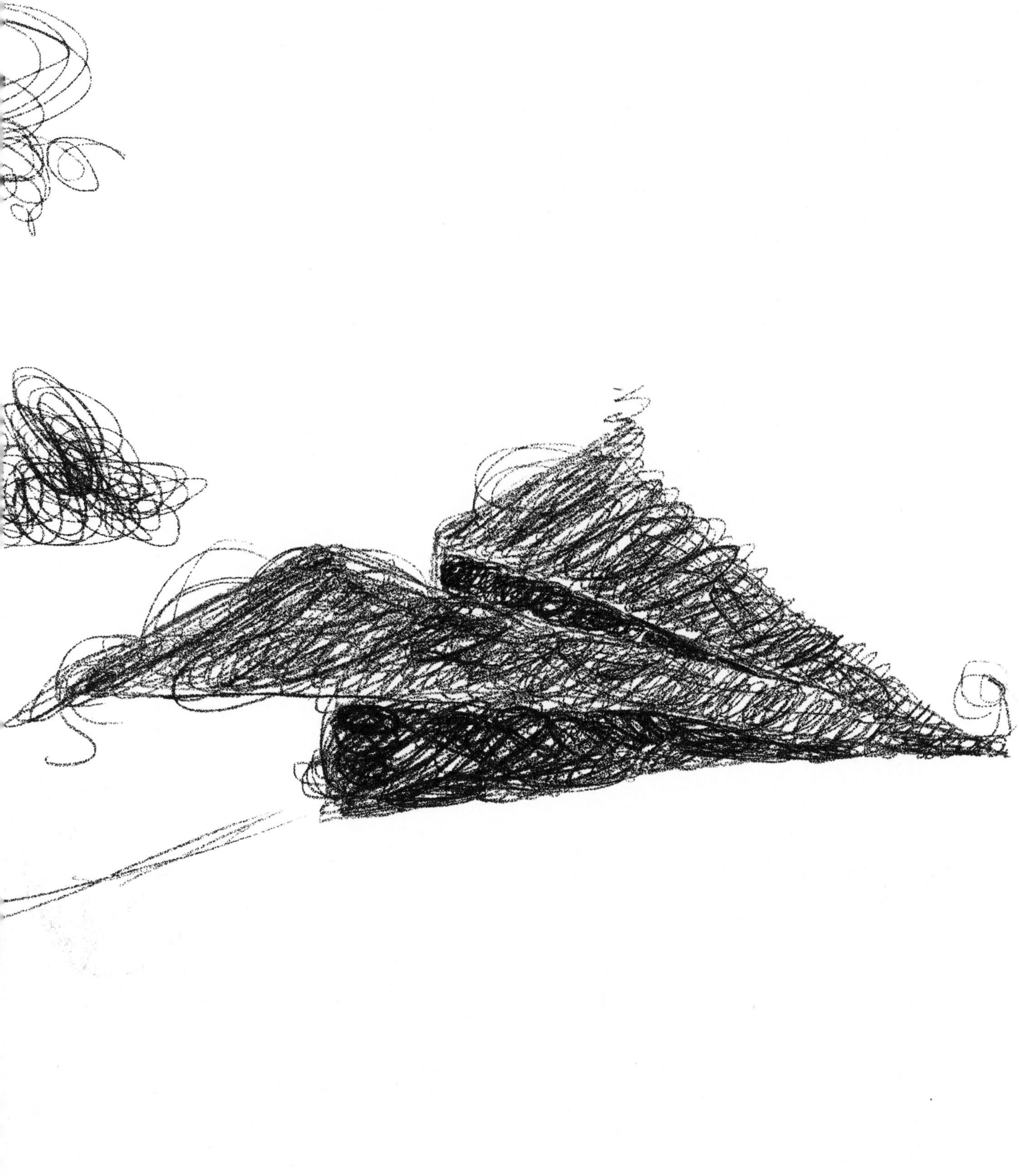

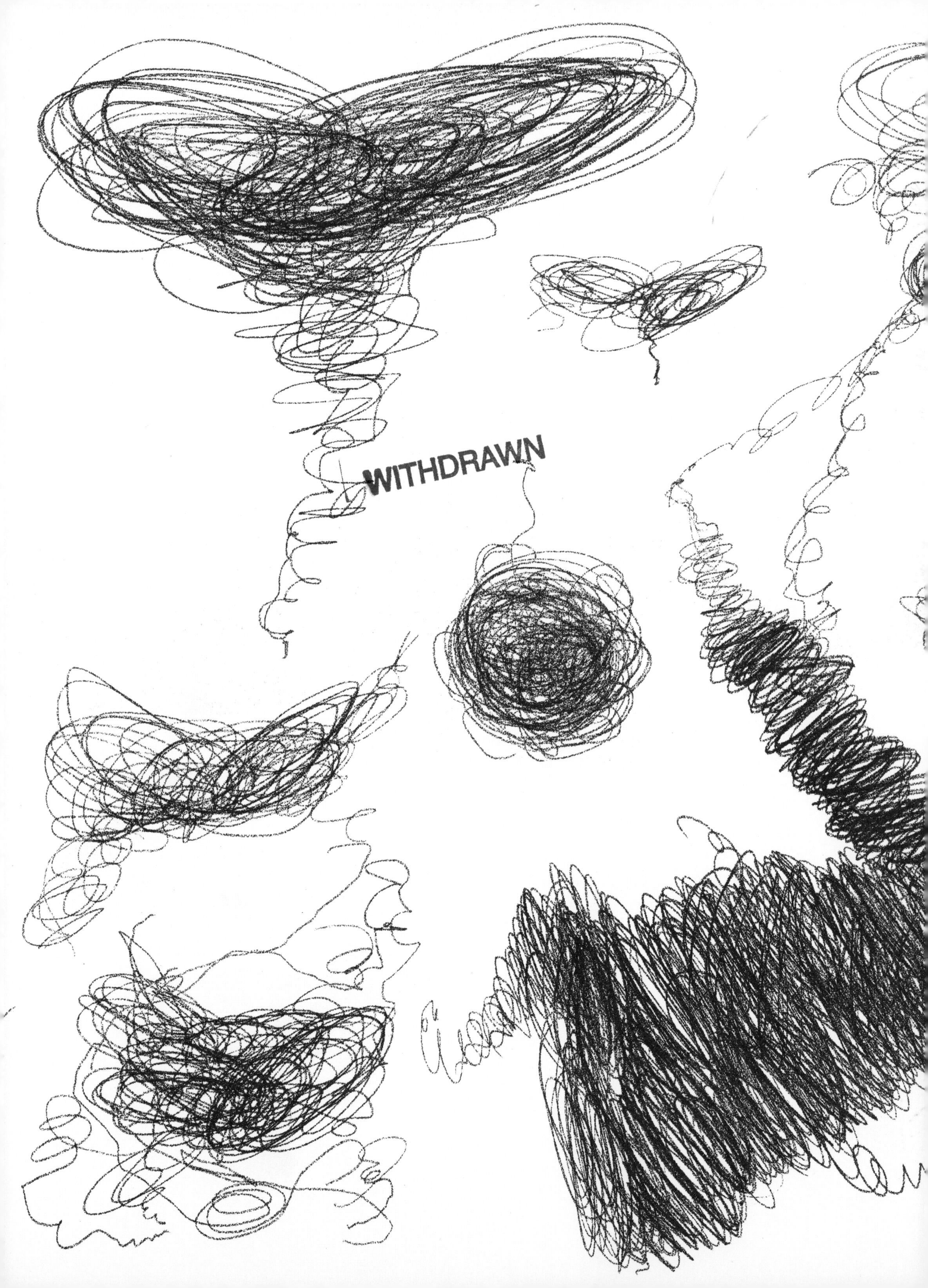